Cultur:
P

D1685228

The High Plains Killings

Chato, a notorious comanchero chief, brutally slaughtered some sodbusters on the wagon-train that Luke Culpepper, an ex-US marshal, was guiding across the Pecos in New Mexico. Now Luke was determined to bring Chato and his villainous gang to justice so he took to the vengeance trail.

But in this quest he had only the assistance of Baldy Springer, his mule with a nose for Indians and a washed-out Pinkerton agent.

Soon it would all end in a bitter shoot-out with Luke's life hanging by a thread and justice no more than a hope.

The High Plains Killings

ELLIOT CONWAY

A Black Horse Western

ROBERT HALE · LONDON

© Elliot Conway 2002
First published in Great Britain 2002

ISBN 0 7090 7042 X

Robert Hale Limited
Clerkenwell House
Clerkenwell Green
London EC1R 0HT

Typeset by
Derek Doyle & Associates, Liverpool.
Printed and bound in Great Britain by
Antony Rowe Limited, Wiltshire.

For Dawn, Paul, Beth, David
and the critter, Rosie

ONE

Luke Culpepper settled back in his saddle opining it was time he got the wagon-train rolling again. He had taken on the job as wagon boss for the twelve German families who had been left stranded at Fort Riley, Kansas after their original wagon boss had got himself shot dead in a saloon, for accusing one of the men he was playing poker with of being a four-flushing cheat.

The Germans, all farmers, were on their way to their new holdings at Carlsburg, on the west bank of the Pecos, New Mexico, and being that he was heading for Texas, it would be a chance to earn some extra cash – which wouldn't come amiss, as he was figuring to start a new life. Luke smiled to himself. As well as being well paid, the Germans had seen him well fed. And it was certainly a heap safer and easier on the nerves than his four-year stint as a US marshal.

He had worked out of Fort Smith, Arkansas, serving papers on bad-asses defying the law in the Nations, for 'Hanging' Judge Isaac Parker. He had bullet and knife scars, and lumps of lead still in his body, showing how dangerous a calling it was. Eventually, Luke decided he'd had a bellyful of cold camps and cold beans for sustenance, and the stomach-tightening strain of having to be always on the alert in case some wanted man bushwhacked him; he handed in his badge.

He decided to go back to his home state, Texas, where he hoped he could get a job as a marshal's deputy in some dead-dog town well away from any cattle trail so he wouldn't be up most of the night cold-cocking rowdy drunk trail-hands and hauling them off to the jailhouse, or throwing down on a man who fancied himself as an up and coming pistolero. If that didn't pan out, he would work the strip of land left to him by his late pa.

Luke rode slowly along the wagons, checking the families in each Conestoga. He didn't want to leave any sodbuster lying drunk on the floor of some saloon here in Monahan, their last halt for supplies in Texas. He had guided his charges this far without any setbacks or trouble and he wanted to keep it that way.

By following the well-used Chisholm cattle-trail south, Luke had brought the wagons safely across the wild, lawless territory of the Nations. Then, by travelling west across Texas, along the route of the Butterfield stage line, running between a line of army posts, the train had made it to Monahan without having had to fire a shot to defend itself. Now he had to lead the wagons north, along the Pecos. Then it could mean earning his due. As a Texan, he was well acquainted with the West Texas saying of there being no law west of the Brazos and no God west of the Pecos.

Luke rode back to the head of the train at a steady trot, calling out as he passed each wagon, 'We're movin' out in five minutes.' He drew up his mount to wait until the families had finished strapping on all their cooking pots and pans on the sides of their wagons. When he was satisfied everyone was ready, he raised his hat above his head and yelled, 'Let 'em roll!'

He heard the sharp cracks of whips and guttural German shouts and, with the rattle of pots and pans and creaking wheels the wagon train rocked into movement. Luke waited until all the wagons had rolled past him, nodding back at the smiling, hand-waving children alongside the wagons before riding out ahead of the train, clear of the dust clouds it raised in its passage. He rode straight-backed, eyes alert, Winchester laid across his saddle horn, ready for quick use.

TWO

Luke reckoned he had done a good job of nurse-maiding the Germans, calculating that another half-day's trailing and the sodbusters should be bouncing over the soil they had trekked all the way West to plough. Noting no signs of any large bodies of riders, shod or unshod, he relaxed his guard slightly and began to contemplate his plans for the future.

Suddenly his mount gave a coughing snort and stopped dead in its tracks. Luke's brain had only time to register the sight of two arrows sticking out of its neck, when he gasped out in pain himself, as an arrow plunged deep into the fleshy part of his right shoulder causing him to lose his grip on the reins. Then with blood gushing out of its mouth, the horse collapsed beneath him, throwing him sideways out of his saddle.

Luke hit the dirt hard and painfully and was powerless to stop himself rolling down the bank. Every spin of his body drove the snapped short arrow deeper into his body and he plunged into the Pecos barely conscious. The ice-cold waters cleared his pain-fogged brain enough for him to hold his head above the swirling water as he was carried, cork-screwing in the eddies, downriver.

Gasping for breath, numbed by the cold, almost ready to give up the agonizing struggle of staying afloat, the current swept him on to a small, sandy, weed-covered spit of land close to the left bank. Exhausted with pain and loss of blood, he could do no more than struggle a few feet on to the island and, with the river tugging at his legs, passed out.

Two ranch hands looking for strays saw him lying there. By using their ropes as life-lines they waded into the chest-high water and hauled him to safety. Strapping him on to one of their horses, they high-tailed it back to the ranch, keen-eyeing all around them for signs of the men who had arrow-shot the stranger.

THREE

Luke came to lying on a cot in what he took to be a ranch bunkhouse, with bandages strapped tight across his shoulder. It felt as though a branding-iron had seared its mark in his flesh and a dull pain throbbed incessantly in his right leg. The rest of his body ached as though he had been kicked hard several times. He groaned as he tried to lever himself up in the cot and with a gaze blurred by tears of pain he saw an elderly ranch hand wearing a cook's well-stained apron, stoking up the pot-bellied stove in the centre of the room with logs of wood.

On hearing Luke groan, the cook glanced across at him then poured out a cup of coffee from a smoke-blackened pot.

'I reckon you could do with a drop of this,' the old man said, as he came up to the cot. He grinned at Luke. 'I've put in a slug of the hard stuff I keep in the cookhouse just to ease my achin' joints. You're bound to be more than a mite sore; I had to dig deep to get that arrow head outa your arm. And

13

you've got a lump tore out of your right leg by another feathered stick. But you ain't runnin' no fever so it looks as though your wounds ain't about to go bad on you.'

'How long have I been lyin' here, mister?' Luke asked worriedly. 'I was actin' as wagon master for some German sodbusters headin' for their new holdings just north of here when those goddamned Injuns jumped me. Are they OK?'

Luke saw his answer mirrored in the old cook's eyes before he spoke. And Luke wished he had drowned in the Pecos.

'Most of 'em are, Mr Culpepper,' replied the old man. He grinned at Luke's surprised expression. 'Those sodbusters told us who you were. You bein' hauled out of the Pecos, arrow shot and brought here warned the boss that killin' trouble was happenin' on Bar X land so he quickly rounded up the crew and headed upriver loaded for bear.' The cook's face hardened. 'We managed to drive off the comancheros before they massacred all the Germans; shot dead some of the murderin' sonsuvbitches as well. That was two days ago, Mr Culpepper.'

'Comancheros?' Luke said. 'I thought it must have been Injuns who bushwhacked me, seein' I got an arrow stuck in my hide.' He sank back on the cot, the whiskey-laced coffee forgotten, his mind a deep pit of black despair. His carelessness had got women and children killed.

'Naw, it Chato's comancheros who jumped you, Mr Culpepper,' the cook replied. 'Though he is part Injun, as are most of the bloodthirsty scum who ride

14

with him. You were meant to be killed silently so as not to warn the Germans they were headin' slap bang into an ambush. Chato likes all the edge before he makes his move. You ain't the first man by a long chalk Chato's sneaked up on unawares. He's one cunnin' sonuvabitch. Why, there's a whole company of horse soldiers tryin' to hunt him down. All they've done so far is ride round in circles lookin' up each other's asses.'

The old cook's words didn't comfort Luke any. He still believed he had let down the people who had hired him to lead them safely to their new homes. He and no one else was responsible for the deaths of those who lay in shallow graves on the banks of the Pecos.

'That m'be so, friend,' replied Luke. 'But it some-how don't ease my conscience any. I feel it's kinda beholden to me, like the Good Book states, to get blood for blood. I know it won't bring back those folk the comancheros butchered, but I'll sleep more restful if I can send some of those comancheros to Hell where they belong; Chato in particular.' He favoured the old cook with a wry grin. 'I reckon you must think I'm loco intendin' to go off on a wild-ass hunt, but right now I couldn't put my mind to do anything else.'

The old cook grunted non-committally. He wasn't about to waste his breath arguing with a crazy man who admitted the dangerous foolishness of his actions to try and ease an unsettled conscience. He opined that Chato would soon have another scalp hanging from his belt.

'It ain't my place to put a fella off what he reckons he oughta do,' he said. 'But what you're figurin' to do will have to wait until that shoulder of yours mends. The boss don't mind you stayin' on the spread until you're fit enough to travel. Now get that coffee down you and sleep some, that's the only medicine I can give you, bein' I can only doctor horses when I ain't cookin' for hungry, thankless cowhands. And I should be over in the cookhouse right now. If there ain't any grub on their plates the crew will blow my ears off.'

Luke drank the coffee, the whiskey it contained relaxing him enough to lie back and drop off into a light sleep enabling him to forget for a while about the fearful task he had set himself.

FOUR

Baldy Springer heard his mount give a nervous snort. He spat a stream of brown juice between the pricked-up ears of the rangey-legged mule.

'You've got a smell of Injuns passin' this way as well, Jethro,' Baldy said, mockingly. 'You must be gettin' old. I picked up their sign as we were crossin' the trail leadin' into Emory Pass.'

Baldy cast an apprehensive glance over his shoulder at the saw-toothed peaks of the Black Ridge mountains filling the horizon behind him. He took off his hat and scratched at the puckered, fish-belly-coloured skin that covered his hairless head like a macabre skull cap.

'Though they ain't Injuns, Jethro,' he said. 'The tracks I seen were made by iron-shod horses, but too many of 'em to be a ranch-crew's trail.' Baldy's face screwed up in concentration. 'If they ain't Injuns' or cowhands' doin', Jethro,' he said softly, 'those tracks must have been laid down by a big bunch of comancheros headin' north to their hole-up on the Staked Plains. Though your nose ain't playin' you

17

wrong, those sonsuvbitches are as close to Injuns in
their murderous ways and habits as to be blood kin.
And I don't mind confessin', I'm as skeered as you
are knowin' we've just missed bumpin' into them
head on.'

Jethro broke wind, loud and foul.

'You can keep your goddamned opinions to yourself, you, you, walkin' fleabag,' Baldy growled. 'You
oughta be skeered; if the comanchros took you
they'd eat you in a bad winter.'

Jethro snorted.

'I see 'em,' Baldy said. 'I m'be old but I ain't
blind.'

The dust the pair of them had seen was heading
in their direction, too big and slow-moving to have
been raised by an Indian or comanchero war band.
It could only be some of Charlie Goodnight's cattle
being driven to new grass along the Pecos, Baldy
thought. Though he did wonder why they were
being driven so fast. If the hard men Goodnight had
on his payroll didn't shoot him on sight for riding
across their boss's range uninvited, he maybe could
beg some coffee and beans from their cook.

'We'll stay put here, Jethro,' he said. 'Smilin' real
purty to let those trail hands see that I ain't a lookout for some gang of cattle-lifters.'

Ed Newton, riding point on the herd, saw the
lone horseman up on the ridge. Suddenly it didn't
seem like easy-raised wherewithal for him and the
boys, sneaking off with a few score head of longhorns from Charlie Goodnight's vast herds spread
all across southern New Mexico, then driving them

across the line into West Texas where buyers didn't ask for bills of sale.

If the man up ahead was one of Goodnight's crew they would have to leave the cattle and hightail it back to Texas before the watcher raised the alarm – or risk choking on the end of a rope slung across a branch of the hanging tree, or shot dead. Newton stopped his cursing and dirty-mouthing in mid-flow. The rider hadn't cut and run for it, and he couldn't see dust being raised by riders coming in fast to join him, so he figured the man must be a lone drifter. Whoever he was he would have to be got rid of, being as he could describe their likenesses to Goodnight and the old bastard's cattleman's law ran a wide loop, right across into Texas.

'Gino!' he yelled to the left swing rider. 'While I go ahead to have words with that fella, you circle around him, real easy like till you get close enough to cut him down.'

Baldy sat back in his saddle, face fixed in a jaw-aching, guile-less smile. Then his face tightened as he noticed the left-hand rider, a Mexican, was edging his mount round to come on to him from his rear. And seeing the bandolier of reloads slung over one of his shoulders also disturbed Baldy. No dollar-a-day trail hand could afford to buy as many shells, or be foolish enough to allow his hard-working cow pony to carry the extra weight. Alarm bells began to sound in Baldy's ears. If the Mexican wasn't a vaquero he could only be part of a border cattle lift-ing gang. That meant, he reasoned, there was more in the two riders' purpose than just coming across to pass the time of day with him. It would be hot lead not coffee and beans they would hand out.

Baldy had spent most of his life on the high plains of Montana and Wyoming stamping ground of the Sioux and the Crow, trapping for beaver and killing cattle predators for the ranchers. Territory where a man had to develop several senses he hadn't been born with, or lay claim to an early grave.

He had drifted south to New Mexico where there were ranches and townships, Where an over-the-hill old man whose reactions were slowing down could sleep at night with both eyes shut. Or so he had thought.

A lone Apache buck, slipping off the agency and looking for a horse and guns so he could ride south into Mexico to join up with other broncos, jumped him while he was asleep, within a couple of rifle shots from Hondo. Baldy couldn't understand why the Apache hadn't killed him before scalping him, but the Indian's action had saved his life and got his attacker dead.

The fierce agony of the knife sawing away at the top of his head brought him fully awake, mad angry with fear and pain. He had grabbed for his own knife, stuck in the ground at his side, and slashed wildly behind him, disembowelling the Apache. Almost blinded by the blood and the flap of skin and hair hanging down in front of his eyes he left all his gear and scrambled on Jethro's back and made it to Hondo.

Baldy hadn't needed the doctor who treated his wound to tell him he was lucky to be alive. He also told him he could kiss goodbye to his hair ever growing back on his head. Losing his hair didn't upset Baldy any, if it had grown it would have turned white. His close, painful brush with the Grim Reaper had rewakened his instincts of self-preservation and once more he slept on his back with one eye open.

Baldy had both eyes wide open and all senses fully active and smelt trouble, killing trouble, riding in on him. Still smiling, he drew aside his coat and reached inside his shirt, gripping the butt of the Dragoon Colt and thumbed back the hammer to full cock.

Newton relaxed somewhat on seeing who it was sitting up on a raw-boned mule, an old saddle-tramp wearing a long, mangey buffalo-hide coat. Downing him should present no problem. He thin-smiled. The dirty old goat was long overdue for despatching.

The Mexican was the biggest danger, Baldy calculated. If he got behind him the sons-of-bitches had him boxed in. He took a last confirming look at the two riders to make sure his instincts weren't playing him wrong and he wasn't about to gun down two hard-working trail hands.

Baldy's assaying didn't take long, he'd had killing looks cast his way more than once. He cursed. This was trouble he hadn't sought. If he did manage to shoot the Mexican and his *compadre*, he thought, how could he possibly hold off the four, five men with the cattle? He sure couldn't outrun them on Jethro. The old fleabag wouldn't race a gallop short of lighting a fire beneath his ass.

The Mexican was still more than a fair distance

away for the certainty of a killing shot with a pistol but Baldy couldn't let his doubts delay his action any longer; at any moment the Mexican could pull out his rifle and blow him out of his saddle. In a single fluid movement he yanked out the Dragoon, laid the barrel across the crook of his left arm, then took a quick sighting on his target and squeezed off two shots.

In spite of his age and the speed of his action, Baldy had the grim satisfaction of knowing he had lost none of his skill as a marksman. The heavy calibre shells struck Gino full in the chest, tearing his heart apart before blowing fist-size bloody exit holes in his back. The smashing impact of the shells knocked him backwards out of the saddle and, with arms out-flung, he hit the dirt, already a dead man.

The deadly swiftness of the old man's pistol work threw Newton off balance for a few seconds; vital, lost forever seconds, allowing Baldy to twist in his saddle and throw down on him. The last thing Newton saw as he slumped across his horse's neck with a red-weeping hole in his forehead, was the gun flash of the shot that killed him.

Baldy didn't give the two bodies more than a cursory glance, whether they were dead or not didn't matter; they were no longer a threat to him. It was getting-to-hell-out-of-it time, and fast. He pulled Jethro's head round sharply, and dug his heels hard into the mule's ribs.

'Run, you son of Satan!' he yelled. 'Or you'll be gettin' a new owner! And he'll not be as kind-hearted towards you as me!'

Jethro drew back his top lip, baring yellow fangs of teeth in an angry, hurt snarl. He had never been kicked before, and sensing the fear of his owner was shocked into action. With a dirt-and-stones-raising, kicking-back-legs start, almost unseating Baldy, Jethro took off in a headlong gallop.

Although he was raising the dust, Baldy wasn't running scared; he opined he was carrying out what the army big brass would call a strategic withdrawal. He knew the *compadres* of the men he had shot would be out for his blood, seeking revenge, or more likely, he thought, to stop him from alerting the ranch hands at the nearest branding camp that some of their boss's cattle were being lifted.

Baldy had an eye for the terrain and how to use it to his advantage. The slight rise half a mile or so ahead would be where he would make his stand. With the big Sharps rifle that could bring a buffalo to its knees at 500 yards he could maybe make the sons-of-bitches keep their distance until nightfall. As an old trapper and trail breaker the darkness would be his ally. Only an Indian would be able to track him. Even the clumsy-footed Jethro could cover the ground silently in the dark, if pressed to do so.

The five rustlers with the herd had bunched up to watch Newton and Gino closing in on the rider. That the man would have to be killed didn't upset them any; taking precautions to protect their own lives came first.

The sudden killing of their *compadres* had them all rocking back in their saddles with disbelieving looks twisting their faces. Then they got over their shock

23

and began cursing at the fast disappearing shooter. Winchesters were pulled out, heels dug savagely into horses' ribs and they raced after the man who could see them all hanged unless they gunned him down.

Baldy pulled hard on Jethro's reins as the mule breasted the rise, bringing him to a haunch-sliding halt. Before the dust of Jethro's sudden stop had settled, Baldy was out of the saddle, gripping the .50 calibre Sharps single-shot rifle. He slapped Jethro on the rump which sent the mule trotting a few yards down the slope so it was below the rim line, safe from any shots meant for him. Then he dropped flat to the ground behind the ridge.

Baldy laid a handful of shells alongside him and deftly thumbed a load into the Sharps. He took a quick look at his pursuers, coming at him in a loose half-circle, judging their distance, before bringing the Sharps up to the firing position. He raised the back sights and framed the nearest rider in them. He smiled grimly; the cattle-lifting bastards were about to hear the bells of Hell toll.

The deep boom of the buffalo gun and the blood-chilling whine of its shell's flight echoed across the plain. Baldy's target felt a moment or two of infinite pain as the heavy ball caved in his chest. The rustler, choking to death on his own blood, lost all grip on his horse and slid out of the saddle off his still fast-moving mount, hitting the ground in a bouncing roll.

Baldy quickly reloaded and picked out another rider and fired, but only winged his man. The winged rustler dropped across his horse's neck, howling with pain as he clutched his shattered left shoulder. His horse veered away to Baldy's left, still raising the dust. Baldy was satisfied with his score so far; he had cut the odds facing him down to three, and slowed down their style. The sons-of-bitches wouldn't be riding in on him in wild Texas fashion, reckoning on stomping him into the ground. Like him they were kissing dirt behind some mound. Though he was still between a rock and a hard place.

He had to hold them off with the Sharps for at least a couple of hours until it was dark enough for him to break off the action and sneak away unseen. He was banking on the rustlers quitting first, putting their own necks before seeking vengeance for him killing their *compadres*. They had a bunch of stolen cattle behind them to be driven across into Texas which they would lose if the shooting drew any of Goodnight's crew to the scene. Then, as well as losing the cattle they could also forfeit their lives.

Baldy lay, watching, listening and sweating.

FIVE

It had been three days since Luke had left the Bar X, his shoulder not yet fully healed, but the urge to get on the trail of Chato ate painfully at his stomach like a cancerous growth. He had thanked the ranch owner and the crew for tending to his wounds and allowing him to share their rations and had ridden out to pick up the comancheros' sign at the spot where they had attacked the wagon train.

Feeling the way he did, gazing down at the rough-made wooden crosses – stuck in the mounds of freshly turned dirt, he was glad the remaining Germans had journeyed on to their new holdings, escorted by a cavalry detail. Expressionless-faced, mad or not, his only task in this life was to kill Chato and, if possible, as many of his men as he could, even if it meant him losing his own life doing it.

The clear trail of the comancheros petered out on the hard, sun-baked ground before he had crossed the border into New Mexico. Luke cursed Chato to hell and beyond. Then cursed himself for thinking it would be a walkover tracking down men who knew every trick there was in hiding their tracks. What he

27

could see of the tracks they were heading north, so riding north seemed the right thing to do. Of course, Luke thought, the comancheros could have swung east, back into Texas, doing their killing there. Until he had clear signs they had cut away to the border, he would continue north. Otherwise he could be going round in circles like the horse soldiers.

The trail swung away from the Pecos and, on breasting a slight rise, Luke saw the longhorns roaming unattended on both sides of the trail, and the dark, crumpled bundles of two men. He opined the dead men were part of the crew with the herd. The rest of the men nursing the cows must be in hot pursuit of the bunch of rustlers who had gunned down the two men in their attempt to take the cattle. Luke jerked his left-hand rein to take a closer look at the bodies.

'You've read it wrong, Luke,' he told himself. The dead men were Mexicans and Luke hadn't seen men so armed up since the end of the war. He knew he was gazing down on a couple of *bandidos*, cattle-lifters. Then he heard the distant sounds of gunfire which could only mean the herd's crew had caught up with the gang of rustlers and were fighting it out.

It wasn't his fight, Luke thought. He would need all the luck in the world to track down and kill Chato; he didn't want to waste any of that fervently prayed-for luck taking part in a gunfight with a gang of border hard-cases. Luke made to cut away from the abandoned herd, then with a 'what-the-hell' smile, pulled his mount's head round in the direction of the small battle. He had handed in his tin star, but opined he still had peace-officer's blood running through his veins and poor, hard-working, underpaid ranch hands had enough grief to contend with trailing ornery cows all the way to the rail-head towns without having to fight off a gang of border cattle-lifters.

Baldy cursed as a Winchester shell kicked up a spurt of dust near him. The son-of-a-bitch Indianing up on his left, was getting too close for comfort, too close for him to raise his head to try and pinpoint exactly where he was before pulling off a shot without risking a slug in his head. And it wouldn't be dark enough to cut and run for it for another hour or so, that's if Jethro hadn't got tired of waiting for him and taken off on his own.

Then Baldy began to think like an Indian. A Sioux buck wouldn't lie scared waiting for his enemy to come in and kill him, he would take the fight to his foe. Reasoning that if it was his day for dying he would do it like a man, on his feet, not like a yellow cur dog, hard-faced, Baldy pulled out his Bowie and began crawling, low-assed, towards his 'enemy' on the flank. It would have to be a no-fuss killing, he thought. The other two rustlers seemed content to stay put, thinking they had him by the balls keeping him pinned down while their *compadre* sneaked in and finished him off with a well-placed shot. Before the bastards cottoned on to the fact that he had sprung their trap and their buddy was lying there with his throat slit he'd get out of this hairy situation fast, on his own legs if Jethro had quit on him.

Luke pulled out his rifle and dismounted. Keeping crouched down below the skyline, he walked up the ridge to drop on his belly and look over the lip. He was within 200 yards or so of the small battle being played out below him and could clearly see all the participants: saw the two riflemen firing on the old man, and picked out another man belly-crawling to outflank him. The old man in his battered plains hat and long hide coat couldn't be a ranch hand, Luke opined. He favoured him being a ragged-assed drifter unlucky in his wanderings to meet up with a bunch of rustlers. Whoever he was, the old goat had made his mark on the gang, two dead men back at the herd and another body lying behind the riflemen. Right now, Luke thought, the old sharpshooter could do with some back-up. He brought his rifle up into his shoulder, drew a bead on his clearest target then squeezed off a shot.

It was a true killing shot. The rustler groaned loudly and dropped his rifle, stretching out his arms as though he had suddenly come over tired and wanted to catch up on his sleep. The other rifleman heard the crack of the shot and his *compadre*'s dying sigh as he was thumbing reloads into his Winchester. Shells fell from nerveless fingers as he realized that the shooter up on the ridge had all the edge. It was running-for-home time. Luke's second shot caught him in the back as he was getting up on to his knees to make a run for it. He gave a painful grunt and dropped down on to the dirt again, as dead as his *compadre*.

The rustler trying to close in on Baldy also didn't

30

favour the odds he was now facing, and sprang to his feet to cut across to his horse, his wild-eyed gaze swinging between the rifleman on the ridge and the man he had been hoping to kill. Baldy got a clear sighting of him and raised himself up from the ground and threw the Bowie, grunting with the exertion. The panicking rustler glimpsed something glinting in the sunlight, speeding through the air towards him. Before his brain could register what it was and the danger to him, he felt a sickening pain in his neck and the warm stickiness of blood gushing down his throat. Suddenly he had no feeling at all, just a dim, distant sensation of his legs folding up beneath him and falling down into a never-ending dark pit.

Baldy, cautiously, got to his feet. Whoever the shooter was, he knew the killing business well. He tagged him as a regulator hired by Goodnight to put paid to the men who were helping themselves to his longhorns. And regulators, he knew, were men not particular of whom they shot down, being paid on a head count of the bodies they brought in slung across a horse's back, men past protesting to Mr Goodnight they were not cattle-lifters. An apprehensive Baldy raised his Sharps horizontally above his head, the plains' sign that his intentions were peaceful.

'I ain't with these fellas, mister,' he called out. 'The sonsuvbitches kinda sicced themselves on me!'

Luke came down from the ridge, mounted up, riding in close to the old man. He thin-smiled. 'You're sure garbed like some border hard-man,' he said. 'But no self-respecting cattle-lifter would be seen dead up on a slab-sided mule, so you can lower that cannon before you bust a gut.'

Baldy brought the Sharps down to waist height, quickly assessing his saviour, whose smile, though friendly, in no way lightened up the bony, drawn-skinned face. It was the face of a man, Baldy reckoned, with a lot of trouble chewing away at his innards.

'My name is Baldy Springer,' he said. He took off his hat. 'You can see how I came by my handle.' Luke flinched at the sight of the fearsome scar. 'But the Injun who gave me the haircut didn't live to boast to his red brethen at their lodge fires about it,' Baldy continued. 'But that ain't here or there; I oughta be thankin' you for pullin' me out of a tricky situation I just walked blindly into. I take it you been hired by Mr Goodnight to do some regulating for him.'

'No, I ain't a regulator, or a bounty hunter, Mr Springer,' replied Luke. 'Though I did wear a lawman's badge back there in the Nations. Just to be sociable, my name is Luke Culpepper.' Then briefly he told Baldy of his mission, the vendetta against Chato and his comancheros. Luke favoured the old man with a ghost of a smile. 'I reckon you could say I'm still in the law-enforcin' trade, though now it's kinda more personal. I know it's a wild chance me findin' the sonuvabitch's hole-up when he ain't out burnin' and killin', but I've got to damn well try.'

Baldy grinned. 'Now that m'be wrong thinkin' on your part, Mr Culpepper. I caught sight of what me and Jethro, there, think were tracks made by a bunch of comancheros at a pass in the mountains. They were headin' north towards the Staked Plains, where, I opine, Chato has his hole-up. Of course, I could be wrong about the tracks, I wouldn't want to send you off on a wild goose chase, but I don't think so.'

'It's worth checkin' out, Mr Springer,' Luke said. 'It's the only lead I've had so far.' Then he began to wonder how a mule could read tracks, but wasn't nosy enough to ask the old man the secret of the mule's special talent.

'You'll m'be do that, Mr Culpepper,' Baldy said, casually, 'if you can convince those *hombres* ass-kickin' it in on us we ain't a coupla no-good cattle-lifters.'

Luke twisted round in his saddle and saw the dust pattern of several riders rein-lashing their mounts, approaching them. Luke's face lengthened with tension. He figured he was on Goodnight's land, and the biggest cattleman in the south-west employed ornery-tempered men; men, who if they thought he and the old drifter were cattle-thieves they would only live as long as it took them to throw a rope over a branch of the nearest tree.

'Mr Springer,' he said, still eyeing the closing-in riders, 'try not to look so mean and lay down that buffalo gun. We're about to pass the time of day with a bunch of tetchy *hombres*.'

In a cloud of billowing, throat-burning dust, the six riders drew up in a rough semi-circle in front of them. Gimlet-eyed, intimidating men, gringos and Mexicans.

'I take it you boys are some of Mr Goodnight's crew,' Luke said, watching the riders for the slightest signs of any hostile movement from them, such as hands pulling out pistols; Then his beholden trail would end right here along the Pecos in a blaze of gunfire for no goddamned reason at all.

Before he could say who he was and why he was here, the thickset man wearing a well-worn, blue, store suit, growled, 'We know who we are, mister. What I want to know is what you two *hombres* are doing on Mr Goodnight's land? Me and the boys have hightailed it from the west range on hearing the gunfire, passin' a bunch of the boss's longhorns and two dead men on the way. And I can see four more men, likewise dead, lyin' around. Now you two fellas just prove to me why I shouldn't have my boys string you up on yonder tree for bein' no-good cattle-lifters. And make it quick!'

To Luke's surprise it was Baldy who did the answering, backing up his words with the big Sharps. Somehow the old man had the rifle to his shoulder and was pointing it at the hardfaced spokesman.

'Pilgrim,' Baldy grated, 'if those boys of yours so much as fart, so help me I'll blow your spine clear across to that west range you spoke of.'

The ranch-hands caught short by the speed of Baldy's action sat tight in their saddles, as unmoving as though hewn from stone. Baldy gave a satisfied grunt.

'I came south,' continued Baldy, fish-eyeing the rider he guessed was Goodnight's straw boss, 'from the high plains territory of the Sioux and the Crow,

34

seekin' a little peace and a restful night's sleep in my old age. And what happened, eh?' Baldy took off his hat. 'This goddamned happened!' he shrieked, angrily. 'Then those assholes lyin' there were intent on killin' me for stumblin' on them drivin' stolen beef.' Baldy favoured the straw boss with a sneering look. 'When was the last time you saw a seventy-odd-year-old cattle-lifter ridin' a mule, a critter that would be hard pressed to make it to the Texas border in a week?' Baldy gave a shrill whistle and a dour-faced Jethro lumbered up from the dip as if to prove his owner's point. 'Why Mr Goodnight oughta give me and Mr Culpepper there a reward for gettin' rid of some rustlers for him and savin' a bunch of his cows.'

Normally, Macey, the straw boss, wasn't troubled with his nerves. He bossed over a wild outfit, men all shades of colour, but the sight of the loco old man's fearsome scar and what the lump of lead the Sharps threw would do to his innards this close up, had his stomach screwing up into a tight ball of intense pain. He could also judge if a man was a blowhard trying to bluff his way out of a tight corner. The old goat pointing the Sharps at him wasn't playing out a bad poker hand; the son-of-a-bitch was holding all the aces, and the joker. Macy knew all mountain men were loco. He opined it was living up there in the high lonesome with the mountain bears and the bare-assed blood-thirsty red men. He was also a man who had survived an Indian haircut, which would make the old man madder than most of his breed. Macey didn't doubt he would kill him. Though

35

trying not to show the mountain man hadn't thrown a scare in him, glaring, he growled, 'Lower your piece, you old rooster. I'm willin' to listen to your *amigo*'s reason for bein' close to a bunch of stolen cows belongin' to Mr Goodnight.' There was a loud creaking of saddle leather as men relaxed on their mounts as Baldy eased the hammer of the Sharps forward and lowered it to his waist.

'I'm Luke Culpepper,' Luke said. Then began by relating to the straw boss of his stint as a marshal for Judge Parker to allay the hardman's suspicions that somehow he was linked with the cattle-thieves. He had the satisfaction of seeing the straw-boss's face softening somewhat. Then stiffening again on hearing about the wagon-train massacre. 'I feel it was beholden on me,' Luke continued, 'to try and get close enough to Chato, at least, to be able to put a Winchester shell into his black, evil heart. Mr Springer has picked up some tracks north of here which could have been made by the comancheros. We were setting off to ride there when we saw your dust.'

Macey opined Mr Culpepper was every bit as loco as his crazy partner. He hadn't a cat in hell's chance of getting within cannon shot of the comanchero chief, and live. But he wouldn't be the first man whose so-called pride and honour had seen him dead. Though in spite of his gloomy forecast of the tall Texan's chances of succeeding in his mission, the loco *hombre* had the right to play out things the way he saw it.

'I wish you luck in your enterprise, Mister

Culpepper,' he said. 'You can get on the trail pronto; me and the boys will tidy up here. There could be Wanted flyers posted on the fellas you shot. If there's any reward money due you can call at the big house two miles west of here, if you swing back this way from the Staked Plains. You tell who comes to the door that Macey said you had to call.' Macey leant forward in his saddle. 'The same applies to you, Mr Springer, if you're still driftin' around these parts.'

Then Baldy surprised himself. Now he was getting old he had a hankering for company more conversational than Jethro. 'Well,' he said, 'bein' me and Jethro ain't doin' nothin' more than wander around in circles since comin' south, and I sure don't want another brush with a bunch of cattle-lifters, I reckon I'll tag along with Mr Culpepper.' Baldy gave Luke a gapped-toothed grin. 'That's if he don't mind an old mountain man as a trail-buddy and that ornery crow bait of mine don't object to travellin' around with a real horse.'

Luke thought that even if the old man had horns and sported a tail, a man who knew Indians would be a good tracker, and the dead rustlers proved he could handle himself in a tight spot. 'I'd welcome another gun, that's for sure, Mr Springer,' he grinned. 'And I reckon you're old enough to know what we could be ridin' into. Now, pard, I'd be obliged if you could get up on that fine piece of horse flesh of yours and show me those tracks you saw.'

Mentally, Macey shook his head, sadly, as the two newly made partners rode out. He had never seen men so cursed with a death wish before. And death would be their lot if the butcher they were hunting discovered they were on his trail. And it would be a slow, painful manner of dying.

SIX

'There they are, Mr Culpepper,' Baldy said. 'Tracks of at least thirty, thirty-five riders, just as I told you. And they ain't more than three days old, or the rain we had earlier on in the week would've washed them out. There's too many of them to have been made by a ranch crew. And they're headin' north as you can see, the way I figure Chato's goin'.'

Luke gazed long and hard at the stretch of loose earth churned up by the passage of many horses. If the tracks had been made by the comancheros, it meant, as Baldy had said, Chato was making for his hole-up somewhere on the Staked Plains. Though unless Baldy could read the sign right up to Chato's stronghold it wasn't much of a lead, he thought dourly. The Llano Estacado, giving the wild high country its Mexican name, was one big piece of territory to search. Though not as big as searching the whole of southern New Mexico, and west Texas where Chato did his raiding. It meant that Chato was up ahead of them, if Baldy was right.

'Could they have been made by an army patrol,

Mr Springer?' he asked. 'Accordin' to the Bar X cook the cavalry are quarterin' the territory.'

Baldy shook his head. 'Naw, the soldier boys ride real neat and purty, in double file. These tracks were made by riders bunched up.' Then noticing his new partner's doubting looks, he said, 'If you're still unhappy about the way I've read the sign, Mr Culpepper, look at the way Jethro's ears are stickin' skywards. For all his darn cussedness this mule can smell Injuns ten miles away, even if their scent's a week old. I reckon Jethro smells the paint and stuff the red heathens daub on their faces when they're about to go on a killin' spree.' Baldy favoured Luke with a cocky smile. 'Now I figure it ain't too wild a thought to consider that Chato has Injuns, or part Injuns ridin' with him.'

Luke made up his mind. 'We'll head north then, Mr Springer,' he said. 'I've no reason to doubt your skill in readin' sign.' He smiled. 'Or that mule's sensitive nose.'

With the Black Ridge mountains hardly two hours' ride behind them, the two hunters came across the first sure, grim signs they were trailing Chato's comancheros. Splashing their way across a shallow creek, they had to skirt around a gunshot-dead cow lying with its hindquarters in the water. Riding up the slight slope from the creek, all-seeing eyed, rifles drawn, they saw the stone chimney standing like some gigantic grave marker in the middle of a heap of charred and smoke-blackened timber of what had recently been someone's home.

'You can relax, Mr Culpepper,' Baldy said, laying his rifle across his saddle horn. 'There's no smoke or heat comin' from those ruins. They've taken all they wanted here, see?' Baldy pointed at the empty corral. 'They were after horses.'

Something caught Baldy's eyes in a patch of long grass and weeds to the left of the burnt-out house. Lifting up the Sharps again, he heeled Jethro into a walking pace across to have a closer look. Luke stayed where he was, rifle at the ready, as if in spite of his partner's assurance the comancheros could come fire-balling up from the creek hollering for their blood.

He jerked ass in his saddle on hearing Baldy's soft but carrying call of, 'They're here, Mr Culpepper.' Luke rammed the Winchester back into its boot and swung down from his horse and rein-led it across to where his partner was standing looking at the ground.

Hard-boned-faced, Luke gazed down at the two bodies lying in pitiful, twisted postures. The farmer had been scalped and his genitals slashed off. His wife, stripped naked, lay on her back, legs drawn up in her last living moments of agony. The terrible gash at her throat, showing dark against the paleness of her neck, told him of the fearful manner of her death after the comancheros had all used her. Mercifully, so he had been told, none of the German dead had been defiled. Any doubts he may have had about being beholden to see Chato dead, were gone. He would try his damnedest to strangle the murdering son-of-a-bitch with his bare hands if all other ways failed.

'Mr Springer,' he grated, 'you're the *hombre* ridin' point from now on in. Use all your trackin' skills; we're huntin' down a mad dog. Use that mule's ears if you have to, but get us close enough to Chato so I can put several Winchester shells in his dirty hide.'

'I don't need to get you in that close, Mr Culpepper,' Baldy said, as stern-faced as Luke. 'My Sharps can send Chato to where he belongs from a mile away.'

They had seen the bodies decently buried and were riding north again, now and then picking up the trail of the comancheros. Luke knew the hard part would come soon. Chato, on nearing his hole-up, would hide his tracks and the old man would get the chance to prove his skill as a hunter. Luke's hopes were riding on the odd partnership of an old drifter and an ornery mule's sensitive nose. Luke thin-smiled. He might as well get down on his knees and pray for a miracle.

Jethro was the first of Luke's new partners to show him he wasn't riding with freeloaders. The trail had swung away from the creek and now on the right of them was a range of low, grassy-topped hills. Luke heard Baldy give a muttered curse, saw him jerk up straight in his saddle, and lift the big Sharps chest high.

'Trouble, pard?' he asked, looking in the same direction as Baldy, at the flat-topped ridges.

'Jethro reckons so, Mr Culpepper,' Baldy growled. Then Luke noticed the mule's ears standing rigid, heard the animal snort as if confirming its owner's statement.

Luke had never acted on a mule's instincts before but he could see that his partner had taken Jethro's warning seriously. He drew out his Winchester, albeit, a little self-consciously, and levered a shell into its chamber. Only then did he see what the mule had been catching a smell of a few minutes ago.

Set against the fiery ball of the sun, squint-eyed, he picked out the dark figures of a string of riders paralleling their trail along the high ground. He saw the Indians drop down from the ridge as if to cut across their path. Out of the blinding light of the sun, Luke could clearly see their feathered lances, and the long, eagle-feathered head-dress of the leading rider.

'Mr Springer,' he said. 'I owe you and that mule an apology. I thought you were ribbing me about his ears playin' him up when he gets the smell of an Injun.' He nodded towards the closing-in war band. 'Apache or Comanche?'

Baldy shrugged. 'I ain't familiar with the get up of the local Injuns, Mr Culpepper,' he replied. He grinned. 'And this bone-headed, walkin' flea bag don't know a Crow from a Comanche, the wild boys all smell alike to him. But I take all Injuns as natural-born white-eyes haters, which I reckon is only fair considerin' the way we whites have lied and cheated in all our dealin's with them. So I try and avoid meetin' up with them if I can.'

'Are they goin' to pay us a call, Mr Springer?' Luke asked. 'Nine to two are favourable odds for any bad-asses, red or white.'

43

'M'be a couple of the young bucks will come at us to kinda test our mettle and to prove to their chief they've got warriors' balls. That is, if we can't persuade them to seek their fun someplace else. Pull up, Mr Culpepper and we'll let them know just what they'll face if they intend liftin' your scalp.' Baldy favoured Luke with another gap-toothed grin. 'They sure can't lift my hair.'

Baldy brought the Sharps up to his shoulder and pulled off a load. The bang of the discharge and the banshee-like whine of the heavy slug in flight rang loudly along the ridges. Luke saw the wisp of dust the slug had kicked up the hillside well above the Indians, drifting on the light breeze.

'Could've took that chief's head clear off,' Baldy said. 'But it wouldn't be wise to rile them more than they are right now. Though it should make them have second thoughts about attacking us. I figure they thought they were still outa long-gun range.' Then reaching behind him he yanked out a sawn-off double-barrelled shotgun from his bedroll. He drew back the hammers and fired off both loads into the air. 'That should give them something to talk over,' Baldy said, as he thumbed two fresh loads into the shotgun breech and snapped shut the barrels. 'Now, Mr Culpepper,' he said, 'I'd be obliged if you could fire off a coupla shells from your Winchester. Then those boys across there will get the message that we ain't easy pickin's.'

Luke, determined to underline that message, fired off half a magazine load of shells in the general direction of the war band.

'Look!' Baldy cried. 'They've got the message, they're headin' back up on to the ridge!'

Luke breathed out a deep sigh of relief. He didn't hanker after a running fight with a bunch of broncos. His fight was with Chato and any luck he might have coming his way he wanted to save for the battle. Luke's hair at the back of his neck, like Jethro's ears, had stiffened up since sighting the Indians, and stayed bristled when he heard Baldy say, 'Of course, we could raise those red hellions again, Mr Culpepper. They're headin' north, the same direction as us. Could be they're meetin' up with Chato on the Staked Plains to get themselves some guns and rotgut fire-water.'

Luke's face twisted in a grimace of a smile. 'What the hell's another nine killin' *hombres*, Mr Springer, when we're takin' on a whole durn gang of suchlike characters?'

'Ain't nothin' at all,' replied Baldy, po-faced. 'I figure Chato don't need any help to see us dead, if that's the way it's gonna be.'

This time Luke's smile had more warmth in it. 'I take it that means you ain't pullin' out of our partnership. I wouldn't hold it against you if you did. Though I sure would have a hard time makin' it to the Staked Plains on my own without Jethro's Injun-smellin' nose.'

'That you would, Mr Culpepper,' Baldy said. 'That you would.'

Jethro snorted and stamped his front feet.

'Now don't get all uppity,' Baldy growled, good-naturedly, 'just because Mr Culpepper here spoke highly of you. You ain't got the savvy to know what you could be ridin' into. Like the wild boys we're huntin', those red devils across on those hills would eat you when the snows come.' He dug his heels into Jethro's ribs. 'OK, blowhard,' he barked, 'let's move out.'

A disappointed Chief Howling Wolf, keeping well off the skyline, watched the two white-eyes cut away from the high ground. He would have liked to have taken their horses and guns and the two boys in his band could have been blooded as warriors by taking the white-eyes' scalps. But he had seen the killing power of the long gun the older white-eye carried: the gun that fired in the morning and killed when the sun was past its height. He had seen the heavy slug it fired kill a running buffalo dead within its own length as far away as seven, eight arrow flights away.

Howling Wolf could not afford to lose any of his small band of warriors. He had dealings with the 'breed, Chato, in his stronghold in the high country north of here. And he wanted to ride into the 'breed's camp with some pride at the head of a war band, not just two of three warriors.

With the gold and silver ear-rings, bracelets and gold teeth, they had taken from the Mexicans they had killed south of the Rio Bravo, he would buy guns, horses and whiskey from Chato. Weapons and horses he would use to attract other broncos who would acknowledge him as their chief.

The chief's nostrils dilated at the thought of all the killing his enlarged war band would inflict on the hated Mexicans and the white-eyes. He drew his mount round and hurried it along to catch up with his warriors.

SEVEN

The trail twisted again, the hills dropping back far to their left. Crossing over a flat, unbroken range where an Indian, scalp-hunting, Luke thought, confidently, would be hard-pressed to jump them unawares. Luke rode along silently and, not wanting to take things on chance, wary-eyed. Although he didn't show it, sitting slumped back in his saddle, smoking a short-stemmed pipe, Baldy would be alert as he was in keeping a watch out for trail dust of any incoming riders.

Every now and again, Luke glanced, unconsciously at Jethro's now flattened-down ears. He grinned. That would set the drinkers rolling on the floor in any frontier bar if he told them he had only managed to hang on to his hair by watching a mule's twitching ears.

He was curious to know how his partner came to lose his scalp, but reckoned it would be a touchy subject to raise, especially to an experienced hunter as Baldy. And again, in the short time he had known him, he had found out that the old hunter wasn't a gabby man, which suited him. He had a lot occuping his mind working out the tactics he would use when the day came when he found he was within striking range of Chato.

'It ain't any good frettin' about how you're gonna play things when you meet up with Chato, pard,' Baldy said. 'You'll find you'll do what is needed when that time comes as natural as this mule of mine breaks wind. Mark my sayso: you'll give yourself belly ulcers doin' otherwise.'

Luke gave Baldy a look of surprise. The old goat must have read his mind; had he Indian blood in him? 'I guess you're right, pardner,' he said. 'But I'm a worryin' man. Though I'll endeavour to hold back that trait until we're breathin' down Chato's dirty neck.' He smiled. 'That won't stop me from keepin' an eye on that mule of yours ears, Mr Springer.'

'You could do worse, Mr Culpepper,' replied Baldy. 'I figure Jethro's ears must have been jacked up real high the night that Injun jumped me. But, of course, it was dark and the old crow-bait hadn't the savvy to bellow out a warning.' Baldy suddenly raised an arm. 'There's smoke away to our left, see it?'

Luke swung round in his saddle, taking several minutes of keen-eyed gazing before he saw the thin column of smoke against the washed-out blue of the sky. He would have to stop thinking that his partner was over the hill; Baldy had eyes like an hawk. He straightened up in his saddle, giving himself a higher horizon. 'There's buildin's there, Mr Springer. Could be a ranch or a farm.'

'We oughta swing by there,' Baldy said. 'Warn them there's a bunch of broncos prowlin' around close by.' Baldy grinned. 'M'be if they're kind-hearted plainsfolk we might be invited to sit at their table and share their vittles with them. I'd have to apologize for keepin' my hat on; I wouldn't like to scare any kids who might be there.'

'It's quite a spell since I partook of a meal I didn't rustle up myself, Mr Springer,' Luke said. 'Though we're more likely to get a load of buckshot whizzin' around our ears as a welcome. All the trailin' we've been doin' has us lookin' like a couple of West Texas stompin' men runnin' ahead of a hangin' posse.'

Sam Turner stopped his ploughing and unhooked the plough horse's reins from his shoulders as he saw the indistinct shapes of two riders in the heat-haze heading towards him. He cursed profoundly but silently, not wanting his son, Earl, clearing stones out of the plough's path, to hear him dirty-mouthing. Another couple of hired guns, he thought angrily, riding in to beg, or threaten him for a free meal before heading north to Fort Sumner to kill for one of the factions in what the territory called the Lincoln County war.

Sam hawked and spat in the dust like a savage Indian. Wasn't there enough trouble for folk in this section of New Mexico – Chato and his bunch of killers, broncos on killing and burning raids and the hard, unyielding goddamned land without a war starting up?

Mr Antrim, a young pistolero, named on the

Wanted flyers as Billy the Kid, who ran a gang of like-minded wild boys, kept the fire blowing hot. When things became too hectic for Billy and his gang up at Fort Sumner they came south, showing up on some small farm like his, banking on their notoriety as shootists to get their meals free.

Sam's face hardened in anger. The incoming assholes would get the message that it would be better for their health if they kept on riding past the Turner place, or face the consequences.

'Earl!' he called. 'Go and get your rifle from the stump then come and stand by me. 'There's two riders comin' this way and they'll need persuading to keep on travelling.'

When the riders came close enough for Sam to see them more clearly, he thought they must be running short of pistoleros in West Texas. The old man in the long hide coat must have had help to get up on that mule. He hadn't the cut of a fast gun but looks, as he well knew, could be deceptive. Choirboy-faced Billy the Kid proved that.

The old man's partner, a tall lean man, was an *hombre* of a different stamp. He had the keen-eyed sweeping gaze of a man who knew when and where to jump if things got out of hand – and when to stay and make good use of that pistol he had sheathed on his right hip.

'It ain't quite the welcome mat they've laid out for us, pard,' Baldy said softly. 'The kid with the rifle looks more than a mite scared, could jerk off a load at us. And the big pistol his pa's got fisted will put a bigger hole in a man`s hide than the Sharps.

There'll be no chow for us on this fella's table.'

'It pays a man to take precautions to protect his property, Mr Springer. This place ain't all that far from the Texas Panhandle and men seekin' easy pickin's could regularly pass this way. And, as I said, we sure don't look like a coupla tree-stump, hot-gospel-preachin' men.'

'If they make a move for their guns, Earl,' Sam said, as the riders drew up beside the plough, 'send them on their way to Boot Hill.' Stepping closer to them he said, hard-voiced, 'The trail north to Fort Sumner is back a-way to your left.' He waved his pistol between Luke and Baldy, scowling-faced. 'This ain't an open house for no-good Texas drifters.'

Out of the corner of his eye, Luke glimpsed Baldy's right hand make a sudden sweeping movement and then he saw the long barrelled cavalry pistol in his partner's hand. The old man didn't favour a holstered pistol so Luke guessed he'd had the Colt stuffed down his shirt. He thought he still had a lot to learn about the staying-alive capabilities of Mr Springer.

'Now, pilgrim,' he heard Baldy say, in a passing-the-time-of-day voice, 'you've got two choices. Either you can take the wild chance that you'll shoot me dead before I blow that fine young boy of yours head off, or you can put that pistol back down your pants and tell your boy to lower his rifle while Mr Culpepper tells you why we're callin' on you.'

Sam did some more cursing. He had cursed more in the last few minutes than he had in a whole month. He had never seen a shirt-carried gun yanked out so fast before. The old goat was more nimble than he looked. The son-of-a-bitch had him well and truly over a barrel. It was crow-eating time unless he was willing to take a gamble on his boy's life. 'Lower your gun,' he told the white-faced Earl, and tucked his pistol into the waistband of his pants. 'We'll hear what Mr Culpepper has to say.'

'Put your gun away, Mr Springer,' Luke said. 'No man enjoys bein' talked to under threat.' He waited until Baldy had stuffed the Dragoon back in his shirt. 'We saw chimney smoke,' he began. 'And thought it was our Christian duty to go out of our way to warn the folks livin' there about an Injun war band prowlin' around that stretch of hills back to the east of us.' He smiled. 'Mr Springer here persuaded them to haul their asses over the ridges.'

'A war band, you say, Mr Culpepper?' Sam said.

Luke nodded. 'Nine of them. Heading north the last sighting we had of them. But bein' Injuns they could have swung this way.'

'I don't think so,' replied Sam. 'My guess is they're still riding north to meet up with Chato and his comancheros at their stronghold somewhere on the Staked Plains.'

'Chato!' said Luke. 'Ain't it a small world, Mr Springer? Why, he's the fella we're tryin' to track down, friend.'

Sam's mouth gaped open in disbelief. 'You're goin' after that murderin' sonuvabitch, Chato? I take it you've got a posse of hard-ridin', fast-shootin' *hombres* comin' in behind you. Then you just might have an odds-on chance of puttin' Chato

54

in his grave. That's if you can find where he holes-up.'

Luke smiled. 'No, I ain't; there's just the two of us. We figure if we're as snaky as a coupla hair-liftin' broncos we'll have a better chance of gettin' close to Chato. Seven hundred yards close is all we need. The big Sharps Mr Springer favours will do the rest.'

'Well, it ain't my business to put a man off what he feels is his duty,' Sam said. He would have liked to know how that duty was come by but it wasn't polite to ask. 'But if I was contemplatin' suicide,' he added, 'I could never pick a surer way.' He gave them both a pitying look. 'And if you don't mind takin' some advice from a stranger, I'd swing further east, towards the Pecos, before headin' north to the Staked Plains, or you'll hit big trouble sooner than you expect. It's open season for shootin' at newcomers ridin' into Lincoln County. Two factions are warrin' up there for some reason or other. Some of them mere kids.'

'We'll take heed of that warnin',' Luke said. 'We don't aim to fight our way up to Chato's front door.'

No, thought Sam, coldly. If you make it to Chato's camp you and your pard will get all the fighting you can handle, and then some. He snapped his fingers as he remembered something. 'There's an *hombre* I know who might be of some help to you in trackin' down Chato. That's if you can persuade a man who is loco to talk to you.'

'As I said, I'll accept anyone's help,' Luke replied, 'if it gets us within shootin' distance of Chato. I take it this loco fella don't hold any good feelings for Chato.'

'I'd put it stronger than that, Mr Culpepper,' Sam said. 'The "Mole", we call him, seein' as he ain't told us his real name; he don't talk much, but when he does, he heaps curses on Chato's head and shows us the rope burn round his neck. He drifted down here about six, seven months ago, a half-crazy walking dead man, and made camp at Silver Butte, a worked-out old mine three miles north of here, existin' on what he could trap and dig out of the ground. Then he started scratchin' for silver in the mine. The few bits he gets he trades with the agency Apache for what scraps of food they can spare. The Apache use the silver to make fancy geegaws for their squaws.

'Every now and again,' Sam continued, 'me, or my boy, take him some fresh bread or whatever Ma's baked. He tells us he's diggin' for the motherlode.' Sam laughed. 'And I've cash in the bank. I think it's the Mole's way of occupyin' his mind to stop him thinkin' about what happened to him where he came from.'

'It won't do no harm talkin' to this Mole *hombre*,' Luke said. 'Ain't that so, pard?'

Baldy grinned. 'He oughta want to chat with two more crazy men, I reckon.'

Sam watched them ride out, having no doubts in his mind that Mr Culpepper and Mr Springer were living on borrowed time unless they forgot their foolish notion of hunting down Chato. Which would be a pity, he thought, the pair seemed decent, law-abiding gents. He picked up the reins. 'Let's get this ploughin' finished, Earl, Ma will be shoutin' us in for supper soon.'

EIGHT

'That must be Silver Butte, Mr Springer,' Luke said nodding towards the dark-faced mass of rock standing on its own away to their left. Straight-faced, he added, 'I'll let you do the talkin', pard; two lonesome drifters oughta see things the same way.'

Baldy replied in a Jethro-like derisive snort.

The trail leading to the mine was overgrown by grass and sage but they could clearly see the deep ruts in the hard-pan ground of the countless wagons loading ore from the mine and carrying supplies in when it was working full blast.

Campbell MacColl twisted and threshed on his bed of dried brush like a man in the grip of a high fever. Sobbing moans racked his body, as once again he was reliving his nightmares, ever since that terrible day on the Staked Plains when what was torturing his mind now, threatening his sanity, had been a fearful reality.

The physical and mental exhaustion of hacking out of the hard rock the strands of silver from the working faces of the mine with old tools left by the former miners somehow kept his night terrors from taking over his daylight hours and pushing him over the edge into the dark despair of total madness.

Campbell came awake, howling like a badly injured dog, hands clapped over his ears to cut out the soul-destroying screams of his dead partner, and saw three men standing in the cave entrance. The fear sweat froze on his body and the scar round his neck burned as though the rope that had caused it was still choking the life out of him. He gave a dry-throated scream of fright as the men hauled him, unresisting, out into the open.

Baldy raised a warning hand. 'The Mole's already got visitors,' he said. 'And they don't seem very friendly towards him.'

Luke saw the three men dragging the man who could only be the Mole out of the mine entrance, and not fighting against the rough handling he was receiving. As he rode closer he noticed the Mole was aptly named: long, dirty, straggle-haired, hairy-faced, ragged clothes caked in dry mud from the workings, he made Mr Springer, who wasn't particular in his appearance, look as sharp a dresser as a city tailor's dummy. And he could smell him from here and he was upwind of him. His age was hard to determine, but Luke guessed he could give the Mole a good few years.

'Your diggin' is dirtyin' the crick, you crazy sonuvabitch!' one of the ranch hands said. 'Our boss wants you off this piece of land; pronto like.' The ranch hand laughed as he kicked the helpless Mole in the ribs. 'Do you get the message or do you want me to put it to you stronger?'

Luke's face hardened in anger. He didn't know if the Mole would speak to him and Baldy, and if he did it could put him no closer to killing Chato. It was a chance he had to take. One thing was certain: if he allowed the ranch hands to beat up the Mole he wouldn't be in a fit state to do any talking.

His pistol seemed to jump into his hand, firing off a warning shot over the ranch hands' heads. The Mole dropped face down on to the ground, as the men holding him spun round in alarm, hands clawing for their guns.

'Don't even think of it, pilgrims,' he heard Baldy say. The old trapper had his own pistol out, the long barrel laid steady on his left forearm. 'Or your carcasses will be dirtyin' that crick's water.'

Three gun hands stayed their movement.

'This ain't no business of yours!' the man who had been kicking the Mole snarled back at Baldy. 'This is cattlemen's business, and you better believe it. That stinkin' apology of a man lyin' there is on Circle C land and his scratchin' in the old workings is muddyin' the crick, and that water's the herd's drinkin' water. I've orders to clear the bum outta this mine, the easy way, or the hard way if we have to. Now, old man, to save yourselves a whole heap of trouble, I'd advise you and your pard to keep on passin' through this stretch of territory.'

Baldy's Colt suddenly flamed and boomed and the ranch hand who had been doing the threatening cried out in pain and clutched at his right, blood-dripping arm. The pistol he had been easing out of its holster as he had been talking slid back in

61

again. Face twisted in a mask of pain and anger, he screeched, 'I'll see you hangin' from the nearest cottonwood, you old bastard! There'll be ten guns the next time you see us!'

'Some folk don't hear so clearly, pard,' Baldy said. 'Or too durn foolish to heed sensible advice when kindly given.' Luke cursed under his breath; things had turned sour on them. He kept his gun, unwavering on the trail hands, face pale and angular. Would there have to be more unnecessary bloodshed? He hoped to hell Baldy's single shot had made the ranch hands see reason. Yet he knew from his experience as a peace-officer, a ranch crew was fiercely loyal to each other. A wrong or a hurt, to one was an insult to them all. They would back up a *compadre* in any trouble come hell and high water, even if it meant dying alongside him.

He could only pray that the ranch hands, with guns held on them by men willing to use them, would treat the situation as a Mexican standoff and mount up and ride back to their ranch to tell their boss that his orders to shift the Mole off his land hadn't worked out as planned. He didn't think that likely. His talk with the Mole could now only last as long as he figured it would take for the Circle C boss to round up as many men as he could and ass kick it back here spoilin' for a fight.

'We didn't seek trouble,' Luke said. 'All we wanted was to have a talk with the fella you've been kickin' around. And believe me, we've got strong reasons for doin' so. But what's done had to be done and let it lie at that. So my advice, mister, is to get back to your spread and get that wound seen to. What you feel you oughta do next is your business.' Luke cold-smiled. 'Though I oughta tell you me and my pard will be long gone from here if you opine blood calls for blood. And we ain't easy *hombres* to track.'

Still showing his anger, the wounded man snarled, 'You betcha blood calls for blood. You'd better make your talk with this bum real fast because you're as good as dead! Let's go, boys, and get ourselves a hangin' party rounded-up.' He let loose with a fresh string of curses, as, awkwardly and painfully, he mounted his horse.

'If we're talkin' war here, friend,' Baldy said, pushing his pistol down the top of his pants and drawing out the Sharps. 'Don't try any skirmishin' till you get the rest of your army. This Sharps can put a man down for keeps at a thousand yards, so don't let me see any of you boys tryin' to Injun back this way figurin' to catch us off guard.'

In return, Baldy got three 'drop dead' looks and a spoken warning, punctuated by more dirty-mouthing, from the man he had winged, that when they returned there would be nothing sneaky about it. They would come in with a rush, and shooting.

Luke watched their fast disappearing trail dust then said, 'Keep an eye on them, Mr Springer, while I have a talk to the Mole.'

He dismounted and walked across to the Mole who was still on the ground but now sitting up. Through the tangled mass of uncombed hair, he saw a pair of eyes glinting wildly at him. Luke had intended, on hearing how the Mole lived, to probe him gently for information about Chato; he no longer had the time to do that. He didn't know how much time he really had before he heard Baldy yell out that a bunch of riders was fireballing in. His mission to put paid to Chato wasn't about to be ended here just because he had to plead, humour, cajole, whatever, some half-loco man into talking. Tough, fast questioning was called for.

'Mister,' he grated, 'I don't know who the hell you are or why you've chosen to live no better than some wild critter. I only hope you ain't as crazy as you look and you know what I'm sayin'.' Luke saw no sign in the Mole's unblinking-eyed stare that what he had just said was registering in his brain. He sighed and cast a worried glance at Baldy. He saw the old man give a reassuring shake of his head. Time hadn't run out for them yet. He pressed on with his questioning.

'All I'm interested in is what you know of the comanchero leader, Chato. I've heard you knew of him before you came south to this mine.'

Luke knew he had made a breakthrough. At the mention of Chato, the Mole flinched as though he had struck him a blow with his fist and saw the staring eyes widen in fear. He gave a grunt of satisfaction. 'I see that you're acquainted with the murderin' sonuvabitch and it wasn't a joyful meeting. Now I would be obliged if you'd tell me all you know about Chato. M'be give me an idea where the bastard holes up between raids. And make it quick. Those fellas who were roughin' you up will be back

64

with more like-minded gents and this time they'll be that mad they'll see you planted. Now m'be you don't give a hoot whether you live or die, but me and my pard ain't got any death wish. We aim to stay alive and put a bullet in Chato's dirty hide. We're kinda on a blood-for-blood mission.'

Baldy kneed his mount closer to them, though still keeping a watchful eye on the trail. Almost snarling the words out, he said, 'You're beholden to us, mister. We stuck out our necks for you and landed ourselves into trouble we could do without. We could've kept our distance and you would be lyin' there spittin' blood with your ribs caved in – an easy meal for the wolves and wild dogs that must roam around here after dark.' Baldy's voice softened. 'I figure that somehow Chato threw one helluva scare into you,' he said. 'For no white man would live in a hole in the ground like some varmint: unless he was hidin' from someone, or loco.' He took off his hat to show his scalpless head. 'Now the red heathen who did that sure scared the hell outa me, but not enough to stop me from despatchin' him to his happy huntin' grounds, no sir.' Baldy's voice steeled over. 'While you're sittin' there too skeered to even talk about Chato, those ranch hands could be poundin' back along the trail with blood in their eyes. Now that's something to fret over, pilgrim.'

Campbell's mouth gaped open in horror at the sight of Baldy's horrific scar. Then, looking directly at Luke, gasped, 'Kill Chato? Just the two of you?' He gave a croaking sob of a laugh. 'And you say you haven't got a death wish?'

65

'Sometimes a man has to risk his life to get even,'
Luke replied flat-voiced. 'Call it pride, honour or
just plain cussedness, what it is doesn't matter. A
man, if he wants to live with himself has to do what
he thinks right, what he lives by. And my choice is to
see Chato dead. Now tell me about him.'

A flickering spark of anger flared up in Campbell's
chest. 'You never had your partner cut to pieces!' he
cried. 'Heard every single scream as their knives cut
into him until he couldn't scream any more! And I
could do damn all to help him!' Campbell glared
wildly at Luke. 'I still hear his screams. How do you
live with that nightmare, pilgrim?'

Luke and Baldy exchanged significant glances.
'No, I ain't had a partner hacked to death,' Luke
said. 'But bein' a US marshal a while back, I had
partners killed alongside me. I sure didn't blame
myself for their deaths, it was a hazard that came
with the badge. What I felt obliged to do was to go
out and kill the bastards who shot them.'

Baldy favoured the Mole with a hard-eyed look of
contempt. 'The way to get rid of those disturbin''
thoughts of yours, mister, is as my pard says: find
your backbone and go huntin' for Chato and make
him pay for what he did to your pard. Though by the
way things have turned out here you've got a fresh
load of worry and grief comin' your way.' Baldy
jerked Jethro's head round. 'I reckon it's time we
were movin' out, Mr Culpepper, this yellow dog ain't
gonna tell us anything about Chato. And I sure as
hell ain't riskin' my hide to protect him from those
boys we ran off when they come hightailin' it back.'

The angry spark inside Campbell suddenly flared red-hot right to his brain. With a strangled cry he sprang to his feet, fists clenching and unclenching with frustrated rage. 'I'm not a coward, you, you old goat!' he yelled. 'If I had a gun in my hand I'd shoot you off that mangey-hide mule you're sitting on!' Then his body sagged, dejectedly, and tears coursed down his cheeks. 'It was my first assignment,' he muttered, all the fire gone from his voice. 'And I let my partner down.'

'Were you peace officers?' Luke asked.

Campbell shook his head. 'No, we were Pinkertons.'

'Pinkertons? Who the hell are those fellas, Mr Culpepper?' a curious Baldy asked.

'They're a bunch of so-called private lawmen run by an Eastern dude called Mr Pinkerton,' replied Luke. 'I didn't know they operated this far west.'

Baldy gave the Mole a pitying look. Eastern dudes trying to track down a gang of wild, killing *hombres*? Baldy thought even city dudes wouldn't be that loco. The kid's partner had been asking to be carved up. And his threat to blow him out of his saddle if he had been fisting a gun had as much chance of succeeding as he and his partner's attempt to capture Chato had. He was shaking like a town drunk seeking his first pull at the bottle of the day. The Mole couldn't hit him even if he was standing nose to nose to Jethro.

But he had needled the Mole into being angry. There was hope yet for him, he thought. If the Mole got angry enough he could lose his fear of Chato.

67

'If I riled you,' he said, 'I'll apologize, but that's the way me and Mr Culpepper see you. And we can't waste shells on a shoot-out between us, we may need them to beat off those ranch hands we upset when they come ridin' in, if we don't get the hell out of it. Me and my pard ain't hard-assed it all the way north just to exchange lead with some put-out cowboys.'

Luke raised his head and saw the ominous cloud of trail dust of high kicking horses racing in. He bleak-eyed Campbell.

'Are you with us, Mr Pinkerton man?' he said. 'Or are you still a quitter? There ain't no time to enter into a lengthy discussion with yourself to find out what you are. Me and Mr Springer are pullin' out right now. All the fightin' we want to take part in is with Chato.'

Campbell didn't have to do any soul-searching. He looked unwavering-eyed at Luke.

'I'll ride with you, Mr Culpepper,' he said, his voice as steady as his gaze. He knew he was getting the chance to redeem his and the Pinkerton Detective Agency's honour. And somehow he was having the feeling it wouldn't be such a one-sided fight if they did clash with friend Chato and his comancheros. Mr Culpepper and Mr Springer were confident-looking men, capable of giving a good account of themselves whatever the odds.

Luke smiled. 'Good, have you a horse?'

Cambell nodded. 'Yes, it's down by the creek.'

That pleased Luke. He wasn't looking forward to having a man who smelt like a polecat sitting up behind him. He opined even his ex-trapper partner, used to strong smells would balk at having the Pinkerton as a passenger. To boost their new partner's born-again confidence further he said, 'We're right pleased to accept the offer of another gun, isn't that so, Mr Springer?'

'No disagreement from me about that, Mr Culpepper,' Baldy replied. 'You, young pard, gather what bits and pieces you have and get up on your horse, fast. Then you ride out with Mr Culpepper. I'll stay put and try win us some time with the Sharps.'

Baldy's action was sound tactics to Luke. Like himself, the old man had doubts that their new partner, in the state he was in, would be able to stay up on his horse if forced to ride it hard. 'We'll hole-up some place ten, twelve miles north of here, Mr Springer,' he said. 'Where we can get a clear view of our back trail.' He thin-smiled. 'If we can see more than one rider comin' along it, me and the boy will get movin' north again for I'll figure you've either been shot dead, or are swingin' by the neck from some tree.'

'And that would be a durn shame, Mr Culpepper,' Baldy said, ' 'Cos I was lookin' real forward to havin' that sonuvabitch, Chato, framed in the sights of my Sharps, but life ain't always full of good times.'

Luke touched his hat in a salute. 'I look forward to seein' your ugly mug soon, pard,' he said. 'Let's go, kid,' he said, as Campbell rode up from the creek. 'Let the man go about his business.'

Baldy counted eight riders coming in, hell bent, all bunched up. He raised the back sights of the Sharps,

69

cold-smiling. They wouldn't stay close up for long. He lay prone behind a heap of brush-covered mine spoil. On his right side, standing upright were eight reloads for the Sharps, blunt, ugly pieces of lead. It was open ground in front of him so when he opened up with the Sharps the ranch hands would have to burrow into the dirt like prairie dogs for shelter from his fire.

The Mole not being able to stay the pace if pushed hard, thereby endangering Mr Culpepper's life, hadn't been the only reason for him staying behind. His partner, a plainsman, like himself, would use the won time to hide their tracks for the first few miles out from the old mine to throw their pursuers off the scent if his plan didn't work out in his favour. He brought the Sharps up then eased back the trigger.

The shell passing close by their heads and the air-cracking bang of its discharge were clearly heard by the riders, and all reacted to the blood-freezing sounds in the same way. Reins were yanked hard bringing their mounts to an ass-sliding, dust-raising stop that threatened to unseat some of them. Then came the panic-stricken dash for the hoped for safety of the nearest fold in the ground.

Jeb Carlson, the owner of the Circle C spread, raised his head high enough from the dirt to yell, 'What the hell gun is that, Jake?'

Jake, who had landed heavily on his now bandaged arm, stopped his painful cursing long enough to call back, 'It's the big gun of the old goat who plugged me, boss!'

A shell raising a spout of dust in front of Jeb had the ranch boss eating dirt again, fast. Jesus Christ! he thought wildly, we might as well have come armed with staves for what use our Winchesters are at this range, even if they weren't stuck in their boots on the horses. His body gave a nerve-jangling twitch as another shell thudded into the ground close by him. He kept his head low. Twisting it round he spat out a mouthful of dirt and began shouting out orders. After all he was the boss.

'If any of you boys are close enough to the horses make a grab for your rifles! Then, by belly-crawlin', you could outflank that sonuvabitch!'

He had hardly got the words out of his mouth when one of the horses gave a snort of pain as a shell creased its left hind leg, and Jeb heard the drumming of hooves as the horses took off to parts unknown. He cursed. The bastard on the ridge must have read his mind; he was playing with them. Soon he would be shooting for real.

He had to accept the craw-choking truth that, armed only with pistols and on foot they weren't going to show the asshole drifter up there on the ridge a taste of cattleman's law. It would take a troop of soldier boys, armed with repeating carbines, to shift the old man off the high ground, and his boys were only ranch hands. He didn't want their blood on his hands. His mind was read again, this time by one of his crew.

'Boss!' he heard one yell. 'I'm pulling outa this mess! You pay me a dollar and three squares a day for tendin' your cows, and m'be throw a scare in any

71

cattle-lifter who comes snoopin' round the herd. Not for me lyin' here pissin' my pants waitin' for that bastard with his artillery piece to blow a big hole in me! I'll pick up what's due to me back at the big house!'

'Hold it, Steve!' Jeb shouted. 'We're all quittin'! We've got to find the horses before it gets dark or it'll take all night and part of the morning to get back to the ranch. And it will just be our goddamned luck to find the herd has wandered clear to the four corners of the range!'

Baldy saw their low-ass wriggling retreat and sent two more shells winging close by them to keep up the speed of their withdrawal. His grin of relief reached his ears; his bluff had worked. If the ranch hands had had the guts to rush he would have had to hightail after his two partners, or end up as the most wanted killer in New Mexico. The Sharps was a hunter's gun, designed to kill buffaloes, bears and other big game. At no time would he have shot at any of the ranch hands. A man hit by one of its shells in the arms or legs, even at the gun's extreme range would suffer a painful mutilating wound that would see him dead as sure as a shot in the head or heart.

Between watching the trail for signs of Baldy, Luke gave their new partner a closer assaying look. He now knew his name was Campbell MacColl, an Easterner from Chicago. And a great deal younger than he had first estimated, only twenty-four years old, almost half his age. Luke didn't ask how he came to be captured by Chato and the manner of

72

escape from the comancheros' hands. He could see by the way the boy's fingers kept jerking at the collar of his ragged apology of a shirt, exposing the rope weal, he had a long way to go before he got over his experiences at the comanchero camp to be able to speak about them.

Although MacColl had stated he wanted to ride with him as a partner it would be dangerously foolish to rely on his full backing in a gunfight with the comancheros. And in a tight corner he and Baldy would be too hard pressed saving their own skins to watch over a shattered-nerved greenhorn kid. He would be happy just to have MacColl point him in the direction of Chato's hole-up then he could ride off and scratch for silver or gold in some other old workings.

'Will Mr Springer be OK, Mr Culpepper?' he heard the boy ask. 'He's facing considerable odds.'

'He'll be OK,' he replied. 'You'll see the old goat cock-a-hoop on his ornery mule come riding in soon.' That's if things haven't gone wrong, he added under his breath. 'Things had gone badly wrong for Mr Springer once before and it cost him his hair.' He smiled reassuringly. 'It ain't as if he's tryin' to hold back a posse of men paid blood money by some town marshal, Mr MacColl. They're just hard-workin', poorly paid ranch hands. They'll not have the inclination to put themselves up as targets for a gun that throws .50 calibre shells a quarter of a mile, and hurt real bad if you get one in your hide – if it don't kill you stone dead. I reckon. . . .' Luke suddenly broke off his conversation. 'See!' he said,

73

pointing along the trail. 'Here's our pard ridin' in nice and peaceful. So it looks as though we ain't got the worry of a bunch of angry cow-hands tailin' us.'

Baldy's wide-smiling face as he rode up the grade towards them confirmed Luke's optimistic statement: they were no longer being hunted.

'Any trouble, Mr Springer?' Luke asked.

'Nah!' replied Baldy. Still grinning he tapped the butt of the Sharps. 'One shell from this deadly beauty passin' close by a fella's head quickly gets him to rethink his priorities. Those fellas who came ridin' in to do us harm suddenly found that they had urgent work to be seen to back at their spread. The last I saw of them they were huntin' around for their horses.'

'Are you still willin' to ride with us, Mr MacColl?' Luke said. 'You, more than me and Mr Springer, know what sort of hell we're ridin' into. You're no longer bein' threatened so you can go where you please. You ain't beholden to us, ain't that so, Mr Springer?'

'That's so, pard,' replied Baldy. 'We're only glad we happened to be around to be of some help to you.'

Campbell shot them both hurt, angry-looking glances. 'I gave you my word, Mr Culpepper!' he snapped. 'I'll admit I haven't the appearance of a man who can be trusted, but I'll play my part as a Pinkerton agent when the time comes. You need have no fear on that score, gentlemen.'

Luke grinned. 'We've noticed you've kinda let yourself go somewhat. And that's the first thing we've got to put right now you're a full partner. The next town we ride into you can get yourself spruced up. We don't want the sheriff to throw you in his jail for makin' his town look untidy.' There was, he hoped, the chance to see how the kid shaped up on the trail, see if his nerves had returned to normal, long before their showdown with Chato, though he still thought Mr MacColl's usefulness would be the information he could give them about the location of the comanchero camp. The sooner the boy was willing to do that, the sooner he would be showing he was becoming a man again. 'OK, let's move out,' he said. 'And find you that bath house, Mr MacColl.'

It had been three foot-weary, much cursing, hours before all the Circle C had managed to get astride their mounts again and were ready to ride back to the ranch.

'I'm quittin' here and now, boss,' Jake said. 'I'm goin' to try and pick up the trail of those three *hombres*. No old bastard is gonna put a bullet in me and ride away smilin'. And Kurt's comin' with me.'

'It's your business, Jake,' Jeb growled, bad-temperedly. He was tired and hungry and wasn't about to argue with a grown man about what he ought or ought not to do. He bossed over an outfit of hard men, but Jake, a West Texan, was mean-minded as well. He would pull a gun on a man rather than reason with him in a dispute. In spite of knowing Jake's rep as a stomping man, Jeb was getting a gut-feeling that if Jake and Kurt met up with the *hombre* who had scared them with his fancy

75

shooting with his big gun, and his pard, they would run into deep trouble, Boot Hill-type trouble. Which was a crying shame, he thought, for Kurt, who hadn't much going for him brainwise, or he wouldn't be riding with Jake, was one hell of a cow-hand. For Kurt's sake he wished them both good luck, then said as he dug his heels into his horse's ribs, 'Let's go boys, and see if the herd's still in one piece.'

NINE

Luke, Baldy and Campbell lay soaking in hot tubs. Baldy was still wearing his hat, not wanting to scare off the two Mexican boys who were refilling the tubs with more hot water when needed.

They had ridden into Fort Sumner from the east, by way of the Mexican quarter, a mixture of dry-sprung planked shacks and crumbling adobe buildings. The bath house was next to a sutler's store, opposite was a cantina. Judging by the four Mexican women, showing a great deal of their uncovered bodies, Luke opined the cantina also served as a whorehouse.

Pleasuring Mexican females, long past looking as pretty as prairie roses, was the farthest thought from Luke's mind. It was occupied with how young MacColl was shaping up after four days with them on the trail. The hot bath seemed to have relaxed him somewhat, though he had not yet related his experiences with the comancheros. And that was something Luke thought couldn't be put off much longer. He had a lot of thinking to do. Once the kid had had his bath he would see to it he had some fresh clothes, and a haircut. Then he would start the serious business of questioning him.

Luke got out of the tub first and, as he was towelling himself dry, he said, 'You stay put for a spell, Mr MacColl, until I get you some new gear. Ain't no sense puttin' your old stuff back on.'

Baldy gave a crackling laugh. 'If you stroll out to the stores jaybird naked,' he said, 'those *señoritas* sunnin' themselves out there on the porch will think business is about to pick up.'

Campbell, who had never frequented a lewd house, and had no intention of doing so in the future, blushed embarrassedly; yet was inwardly pleased that his partners had accepted him enough to josh him good-naturedly. He could also mark up another plus: his last night's sleep had been undisturbed by his recurring nightmares. Campbell was well aware that the key test of his found-again confidence and reliability to his partners would come when they finally faced Chato and his killers. And, he also opined, it was time he told Mr Culpepper all he knew about Chato, how he was captured by him, and his escape. Then, he knew, confidently, he would lay the ghost of his butchered partner for ever.

An hour later, he was dressed in the clothes, a store suit and clean shirt, Luke had brought in. Luke gave him a look over. 'I guessed close enough, pard,' he said. 'It ain't as though you're goin' to a fancy reception, is it?'

'They'll do fine, Mr Culpepper,' Campbell replied.

'Now I'll go and get some of this hair off; there's bound to be a barber's further along the street. And I'll take my horse with me and find the livery barn, it's got a shoe loose on one of its back legs.'

'That's OK, pard,' Luke replied. 'Me and Mr Springer will be in the cantina rustlin' us up a meal.' He hard-eyed Campbell. 'Then, while we're eatin', you can tell us all what you learned about Chato. It might give us the chance to get a slight edge over the sonuvabitch, OK?'

'I had every intention of doing that, Mr Culpepper,' Campbell replied, firm-voiced.

Luke's gaze this time was somewhat softer, a more satisfied look. 'I think the three of us are ready to walk the line, Mr MacColl,' he said.

Campbell couldn't hide his good feelings. He smiled, for the first time since his fearful experiences at the comanchero camp. 'I'll be proud and privileged to stand at your sides when that time comes, pards. I'll see you both when I get back.'

'Well I'll be damned, Kurt!' Jake gasped. 'We've caught up with the sonsuvbitches! That slab-sided mule hitched alongside that big mare is the mount of the old goat who shot me. I knew they would be headin' for Fort Sumner.' He bared his teeth in a wolf-like snarl of a smile. 'Ain't he in for a painful surprise? Get the horses down into that dip; don't make any sense losin' our edge by lettin' them know we're comin'. We'll Indian in on them.'

'What about the other fella, Jake?' Kurt asked.

79

'The one who caused all the ruckus? His horse don't seem anywhere about.'

'I figure he must be off someplace diggin' another hole in a hillside lookin' for silver,' Jake said. 'But he ain't important: it's the old man I want to be lookin' along my pistol barrel.' He fierce-grinned again. 'I'll tell you this, Kurt, he ain't about to get much older. OK, let's do it. I'll give you time to sneak in by the back door: before I burst in on them at the front.'

Luke and Baldy, standing drinking at the bar, were caught unawares when Jake stepped into the cantina. They thought he was a man who had come in for a drink, or the services of one of the short time girls sitting at a nearby table, until one of them gave out a sharp cry of alarm. They both spun round, hands scrambling for pistols, and found they were too late to make a fight of it – unless they wanted to die where they stood. Baldy cursed under his breath; the son-of-a-bitch he had winged, smiling fit to bust, had the drop on them. He was definitely losing his touch as a wide-eyed, always on the alert, plainsman. His goddamned mule had a sharper nose for sniffing coming trouble than he had.

The cantina walls vibrated with the sound of a pistol shot, echoed by the frightened screams of the girls. Baldy groaned and fell back against the bar, face paling with pain from the wound in the fleshy part of his left arm.

'That's just to give you a taste of what I felt when you plugged me, old man,' Jake snarled. 'And to

80

stop you from yankin' that pistol you've got stuck down your shirt.'

Luke's face was a hard, expressionless mask as he rapidly calculated if it was possible to draw his gun and shoot the smug-smiling bastard facing him before the ranch hand's killing shot put him down. Jake, guessing his intention, swung his pistol on to him. 'Don't even think about it, mister,' he grated, still showing his stomping man's grin. 'You ain't got a chance to make the draw. Show him he ain't, Kurt.'

A cocky-smiling Kurt leaned across the bar and jabbed his pistol hard into Luke's back. Luke's hopes of a mad-ass shoot-out ended up as a narrow-eyed, drop-dead glare, choking over the bitter acceptance that he and Baldy were as good as dead.

Luke knew they were going to be shot; he could see it in the killing look showing on the wounded ranch hand's face. Maybe not here in the cantina where there were too many witnesses to prove they had been gunned down in cold blood, but at some quiet spot back along the trail apiece. One good thing was coming out of a bad situation, Luke thought: young Mr MacColl hadn't been taken. He hoped the kid wouldn't walk blindly into the cantina and make the ranch hands' day.

His other big hope was that MacColl wouldn't do anything foolish if he discovered the desperate situation he and Baldy were in, such as attempting a rescue mission. MacColl had no chance at all to take on and beat two men to the draw, especially when one of them had the cut of a border ruffian. His crazy notion of tracking down Chato to satisfy his hurt pride was about to get Baldy killed, he didn't want MacColl to throw away his life for a cause he ought to have known had no chance of succeeding.

'Tie them to a coupla chairs, Kurt,' Jake said, then winked at his partner. 'I can smell something cookin'; we might as well eat before we take them in to stand trial for cattle-lifting.' He smiled at the whores. 'You pretty *señoritas* can get on with your own business; there ain't goin' to be any more trouble here.'

Luke's worst fears had been confirmed, he had heard for sure his and Baldy's death sentences. The Mexican owner of the cantina wouldn't put himself out reporting a shooting in his bar if it seemed that two gringo cattle-thieves had been captured by lawmen.

Campbell glanced at himself in the barber-shop's mirror. In spite of looking pale and haggard with his beard shaved off and hair cut short, he had the pleasant, warm feeling of a man who had returned to the land of the living. A dedicated Pinkerton once more, ready, he believed, to face the dangers of his chosen profession, undaunted.

On nearing the cantina, Campbell noticed two horses tethered in a nearby hollow. They could be the mounts of a couple of ranch hands passing through Fort Sumner. If so why were they partly hidden by the brush in the hollow? And why had he suddenly pulled up his horse without him being aware he had done so? Had he not yet fully regained control of his nerves and it had just been a nervous reaction, or had he unknowingly developed the sixth sense he had been told plainsmen had when danger was close by? Whatever had unsettled him it would be wise to take precautions and prepare for any adverse situation he might walk into when he entered the cantina. As the old saying put it: fore-warned is forearmed. He would be both, Campbell thought.

He removed his gunbelt and slung it across his blanket roll, then, digging into one of his saddle-bags, pulled out a much smaller though heavier calibre gun and holster. Campbell smiled thinly; he had never used the gun and its rig before so he hoped if the worst came to the worst the contrap-tion would work. His smile broadened slightly. When he came to think of it he had never fired any of his guns in his service as a Pinkerton. Campbell kneed his horse into a slow walk the rest of the way to the cantina.

Jake dropped his fork with a clatter on his plate and grabbed for his pistol lying on the table close by his hand when Campbell walked into the cantina. He beady-eyed the newcomer, quickly deciding the pasty-faced young dude was just some store clerk taking time off from behind the counter to have his way with one of the Mexican whores. He presented no threat to him and Kurt.

'Take no heed of those characters roped to those chairs, boy,' he grinned. 'They're just a coupla bad-asses wanted for cattle-liftin' from a spread south of the territory. Me and my deputy are takin' them back to stand trial.' He grinned widely. 'Before the cattlemen take them out and string them up.' He lowered his pistol and picked up his fork and began to eat again.

Campbell got the chilling feeling he had walked into a lion's den. He was getting the chance to prove to his partners he was a man with whom they could safely walk the line, and the line was right in front of him. And so was an early grave. He congratulated himself for preparing for just such a dangerous situation.

More boldly than he was feeling, he favoured Jake with a tight-faced smile and glanced across at the two 'cattle-thieves' as he strode up to the bar. Seeing that Mr Springer had been wounded helped to steel his resolve to do what had to be done. One thing Campbell had painfully learned since riding west of the Pecos, men killed with the gun, knife, rope, without any honour or chivalry. Fair play, codes of civilized combat, were never heard of. Kill any way you could, or be killed was the recognized code in this lawless territory.

Campbell knew he couldn't sink as low, however provoked, as the scum he once had been paid to hunt down, by cold-bloodedly shooting them in the back. Though the only warning the ugly-faced ranch hand would get was the sound of the shot that would put him out of action for a long time.

Luke gave Baldy a despairing look. From some warped sense of loyalty, the kid had come in with some hare-brained idea he could rescue his partners without even being armed. He sure as hell had no chance of sweet-talking the ranch hands into letting them all go; they were worked up for a killing. St

Peter himself couldn't persuade them to change their minds.

Luke saw MacColl stop, half turn away from him as he passed between him and Baldy and their captors. Then his ass cleared the seat of his chair, as far as the ropes binding him allowed, with involuntary shock at the ear-splitting crack as MacColl's right hand spouted flame.

The smashing impact of the close range shot of the .45 calibre Derringer flung Jake and his chair hard against the bar, his good arm shattered at the shoulder, to lie there in a crumpled, unmoving heap. Campbell swung the hand-sized pistol on to Kurt, sitting slack-jawed, pop-eyed, at the sudden and dramatic change in his fortunes.

'Mister,' Campbell said, the rope scar on his neck burning like a necklace of fire with nervous tension. Trying to look and sound like a hard-nosed *pistolero* whose gunning down of men was an everyday occurrence, he said, 'There's another load in this pistol, so don't be so foolish as to make me use it. It'll be a killing shot next time,' he lied.

Kurt had never been a fast, deep-thinking man, not until now that is. He glanced fearfully at Jake lying there, moaning low with pain although he was out for the count. Then at the cold-eyed kid and his little, big-killing gun only spitting distance away from him.

Without another second's thought, he knew what he had to do to protect number one. Grinning sickly, he raised both hands high. Dry-throated with fear he said, hoarsely, 'Kid, I ain't hankerin' to have a lump of lead in my hide, I was only backin' up my pard, Jake, and I reckon he'll be in no fit state when he comes round to carry out what we've hard-assed all this way to do. All I intend doin' is to ride back to the spread and ask the boss for my job back.'

'A wise decision, friend,' Campbell said, still keeping the Derringer pointed at Kurt, well aware that over-confidence could get a man an early grave. 'Now, I think it's advisable to get your friend to the local doc before you head back to where you came from.' He leaned forward and with his free hand pulled out the ranch hands's pistol from its holster and dropped it on to the table. Scowling, real *pistolero*-like, he said, 'If we see so much as a glimpse of you snooping along our back trail then there's more than a fair chance you'll never tend cows again.'

Kurt got slowly to his feet, hand still grabbing air. Casting a lick-lipping, nervous glance at Luke and Baldy, he said, 'You'll never see me again, gents, and that's the gospel truth.' Bending down he hoisted the unconscious Jake across his shoulder, shuddering as he felt the warm stickiness of his partner's blood seeping through his shirt and on to his skin. Bowed-kneed beneath dead weight, he staggered out of the cantina.

Baldy managed a painful twist of a smile. 'We've sure got ourselves one helluva sneaky pard, Mr Culpepper.'

'We have that,' replied Luke, also thinking that Mr MacColl clean shaven, hair cut short, looked too young to be risking his life hunting bandits on the

Staked Plains. Then he cursed himself for harbour-ing such foolish thoughts. The kid had just handled a tricky situation as coolly and expertly as any veteran peace officer, including himself. And, by what he had heard, kids younger than Mr MacColl were raising hell around Fort Sumner.

'You did well, pard,' he said. 'Me and Mr Springer weren't long for this world, and believe me, that ain't the most joyful of situations. Though it took one helluva risk walkin' in and facing two men with the thoughts of killing in their hearts.'

'It wasn't all that much of a risk, Mr Culpepper,' Campbell said, keeping the pride he was feeling out of his voice. 'I had all the advantages. On seeing the two horses away from the cantina I accepted that they could belong to riders from the Circle C want-ing to even things up a little. I couldn't check out the brands on the horses to make certain in case I was being watched from the cantina. I knew if they were Circle C men they would never recognize me as the Mole.' He grinned. 'The Derringer had them fooled. Now let's get you loose of those ropes and see to your wound, Mr Springer. How is it?'

'It hurts like hell, pard,' Baldy said. 'But the shell's gone straight through and it don't seem as though any bones have been broken. I'll live I reckon. I'll clean it with a bottle of that rotgut fire water this place sells for drinkin' man's whiskey. Then, Mr Culpepper, it would be wise for us to get the hell outa Fort Sumner. That fella you put a scare in could be tellin' the town marshal that he and his pard have been set upon on by three border hard-cases. The marshal could take a stroll along this way with a bunch of deputies to rope us in. Sittin' in a town jail ain't gonna help us to bring Chato to his early grave.'

'Makes good sense to me,' replied Luke. 'We've run into enough trouble already and we ain't got within smellin' distance of Chato.' He narrow-eyed Baldy. 'Are you sure you're fit enough to travel, Mr Springer?' Straight-faced, he added, 'Me and Mr MacColl ain't about to act as nursemaids to a sick old man.'

A grinning Baldy took his partner's comment in the manner it was meant. 'Why, it ain't but an inconvenience, Mr Culpepper,' he said. 'Back there in the high country I walked over thirty miles with four Sioux arrow heads stuck in my hide. You get me that whiskey and I'll clean up this scratch.' Baldy's smile changed into a suggestive leer, 'Why, if those purty *señoritas* hadn't just run off and we weren't pressed for time, I would have taken one of them through the back and showed her how half-bear, half-wolf we mountain-men are.'

A smiling Campbell took a quick look round the cantina. 'It seems as though the owner has made himself scarce as well, Mr Culpepper.'

'It figures,' replied Luke. 'Bein' a Mex he don't want to get involved in a gringo shoot-out.' He tossed several coins on to the bar and picked up a nearly full bottle of whiskey. 'While I see to this horn-dog pard of ours, Mr MacColl, I'd be obliged if you could stand watch outside for any *hombres* hurryin' this way. It's a damn shame we've got to leave; I was lookin' forward to a proper sit-down meal. After I've seen to Mr Springer I'll look around the storeroom and pick up what rations we can use on the trail. OK, pard, lets get that coat of yours off so I can do my doctorin'. You can't manage on your own.'

A straight-backed proud Campbell stood on watch on the cantina porch. Not doubting any more that he could stand as an equal alongside his partners, however tough things turned out. He grinned as he heard Mr Springer's shouted curses. The whiskey must be doing its work, he thought.

'There,' Luke said. 'That's stopped the bleedin'.' He had tied a cloth he had found behind the bar round Baldy's wound. He grinned. 'It's made a mess of your fine coat, but it won't stop you from shootin' down Chato.'

Baldy didn't answer him, he was taking a generous pull at the whiskey left in the bottle.

TEN

Two hours' ride east of Fort Sumner, Luke called a halt and made camp on a rocky, windswept ridge which not only gave them a clear sighting of the Fort Sumner trail but a vast stretch of the arid, treeless territory of the Staked Plains, north and east of them.

'Do we risk a fire, Mr Springer?' Luke asked as they tied up their horses to stout growths of brushwood. 'This is Chato's home ground; the sonuvabitch and his wild boys could be bedded down behind some nearby ridge, nearer than we reckon. It ain't wise from now on in to take chances.'

Baldy's face screwed up in deep concentration for several minutes as he sniffed the air. 'Can't smell any campfire smoke, Mr Culpepper,' he said. 'And Chato's camp, I reckon, will be a big settlement with plenty of cooking fires.' He grinned. 'And there ain't any of our red brethren hereabouts either, Jethro's standin' there as though he ain't got a care in the world. Though as you said, Mr Culpepper, it don't do to take things for granted. I'll light you a

91

fire that'll make no more smoke than a man puttin'
a match to his makin's.'

The three partners had eaten well of a meal of
bacon, beans and freshly made biscuits, rations Luke
had raked together from the cantina kitchen, and
now, drinking their coffee, Luke opined it was time
their new partner told them what he knew about
Chato and how he had ended up as his prisoner, and
of his escape from the comanchero camp.

'How did an Eastern private law-enforcing agency
get themselves involved in the trackin' down of a
bunch of comancheros, Mr MacColl?' he said. 'How
come your boss, Mr Pinkerton, thought his men
could do better than the lawmen and the soldier
boys tryin' to rope Chato in? They know the territory, but the murderin' bastard still runs free.'

'We were hired by Mr Charles B. Nicholson, a
New York businessman,' Campbell replied. 'His son
and several of his friends were here in New Mexico
on a guided hunting trip. Unfortunately, they were
ambushed by Chato and his gang. Only one of their
party escaped with his life, one of the guides.
Though badly wounded he staggered into Portales,
a small township east of here, and raised the alarm.
All the rescue party found was the ransacked camp,
and the bodies of the Eastern hunting party,
stripped of their clothes and . . .' Campbell s voice
broke – 'and mutilated.

'Not satisfied with the seeming lack of progress by
the estate's efforts to bring Chato to book, Mr
Nicholson, a wartime friend of Mr Pinkerton, asked
the agency to help in tracking down his son's killers.'

Campbell smiled wanly at Luke and Baldy. 'And here I am. Not a very good showing for yours truly and the Pinkerton Detective Agency, Mr Culpepper, is it? One agent, Mr Parker butchered, me well on my way to being mad, if you hadn't given me the chance to come to my senses.'

'Jesus H. Christ,' Baldy said. 'What did your boss expect, sendin' two men, Eastern dudes at that, after the most bloodthirsty sonuvabitch in the whole of New Mexico?' He spat in the fire in disgust.

'There's only three of us, Mr Springer,' Luke said. 'And one of us is an Easterner.'

'Yeah that's true, pard,' replied Baldy. 'But we know what we're up against. Some big shot of a detective sittin' in an office back East ain't sent us here.' Baldy grinned. 'And besides, we're loco.'

'Mr Pinkerton didn't expect Mr Parker and me to capture Chato, Mr Springer,' Campbell said. 'By listening and asking discreet questions we could maybe get a line on where Chato's camp was, then notify the nearest army post of our findings. Mr Pinkerton thought that being just two of us we wouldn't attract unwelcome attention to ourselves. Being Easterners we wouldn't be suspected as lawmen.'

'And this quiet snoopin' around, Mr MacColl,' Luke said, 'didn't pan out as planned?'

Campbell's face hardened into deep bitter lines. 'No, it didn't, Mr Culpepper.' His voice was low and toneless. 'Portales was as good a place as any to begin our searching for intelligence regarding Chato's whereabouts. Portales is an isolated township in the middle of what is ideal territory for comancheros' encampments, or any other outlaws' camps. Mr Parker figured it was more than likely there would be men there who had contact with Chato, possibly to warn him if any army cavalry patrols were in the area.'

Campbell's head dropped dejectedly on to his chest and he gazed unseeing into the fire for several moments before raising his head and resuming his story once more.

'We were right, Mr Culpepper,' he began. 'Chato had his agents in Portales. They must have heard of us asking questions about Chato; we hadn't been discreet enough. One night, as we were returning to our rooms four men attacked us, knocked us out cold before we could draw our pistols. When we came to, we were roped across the backs of our horses and being led, fast, in a northerly direction. The reason we had not been killed out of hand and dumped in some side alley in Portales, we found out later, was that Chato wanted to question us, to find out what type of lawmen we were and whether we were on our own, or part of a posse coming into the territory to hunt him down.'

'So you got to see the sonuvabitch, Chato, then, Mr MacColl?' Luke said. Then, impatiently, he asked, 'Could you find your way back to the camp?'

'Oh, we saw Chato all right,' replied Campbell. 'He's a man of Mr Springer's build but with a face and eyes that would throw a scare in the Devil himself.' The haunting, faraway look came into his eyes again as he touched his neck. 'It was Chato who

94

marked me for life. As for finding his camp, well, as I said, it was dark and what with being pistol-whipped and the hard riding, I was in no fit state to do much observing. Later, when it was daytime and I was lying on a ledge on the face of a butte, I do remember seeing some features, a peculiar shaped ridge, twin rocky peaks, I would recognize again if I saw them.'

Luke raised a questioning eyebrow. 'How did you come to be perched on a cliff face, Mr MacColl?'

'Chato has some unpleasant ways of extracting information from people, Mr Culpepper,' Campbell said. 'As unpleasant as mine was, I lived through it. Though not by any change on Chato's part, I might add.' Campbell shuddered. 'Mr Parker had no such luck at all. Still hearing his screams as he was being cut to pieces was the reason I ended up at the old mine, working like a slave. Didn't give a damn if the roof caved in on me.' He looked Luke full in the eyes. 'I wanted to die, but I hadn't the guts to put a bullet through my head,' he sobbed.

Regaining control of his emotions, voice firm, he said, 'You and Mr Springer gave me a reason for wanting to live and I thank you both for that. Now I'll tell you why I came to be clinging to the face of a butte, Mr Culpepper.

'On reaching the camp,' Campbell continued, 'we were thrown into a hut, hands and feet still bound.' He gave a wry grin. 'I suppose Chato didn't like his sleep disturbed unless it was a real emergency. Come daylight we were dragged out of the hut to face the man we had been charged to bring to justice. Chato. As I have said, a fearful-looking man, hawk-faced and of mixed blood, every drop of it bad. He lashed us both with his quirt a few times, then he really got down to the business of making us talk.'

Then Campbell told his partners how Parker had been taken away, stripped naked, and pegged out on the ground. He'd had a noose placed around his neck, then, Chato, up on his horse, began hauling him around the camp. 'My bonds had been removed, Mr Culpepper,' he said. 'Chato didn't want me to choke to death before finding out how much a threat Mr Parker and I were to him.' Campbell paused, reliving the fearful events again.

Luke reached out a comforting hand, and gripped Campbell by the shoulder. 'There ain't no need to tell us any more, son,' he said, soft-voiced. 'Recollectin' bad memories ain't the most joyful of pastimes.'

'It's OK, Mr Culpepper,' replied Campbell. 'They're no longer nightmares. I feel the need to talk about them to prove that.'

A stone-faced Luke and Baldy listened to Campbell explain how the lie of the camp had saved his life.

'The encampment was sited in a large grassy hollow on a flat-topped butte, hedged on one side by high ridges,' Campbell said. 'The second time Chato dragged me round the camp, I managed to get some leeway on the rope and slipped the noose off my neck. Still on my stomach I rolled over several times and was over the lip of the butte. It wasn't that I was contemplating suicide, Mr Culpepper. I had the

96

mad idea I could survive a fall down a cliff face and somehow make my escape. If I didn't make it then at least it would be a faster and a damned less painful death than Chato had in store for me.' Campbell looked appealingly at Luke. 'It meant leaving my partner, but what could I do to help him? I guess I was in a blind frightened panic.'

'There ain't nothin' to be ashamed about, Mr MacColl,' Baldy said. 'Your pard was as good as dead. In that situation a man has to look out for himself. Foolishly sacrificin' your life to the enemy is plumb loco. Tryin' to keep yourself alive to get back at the sonuvabitch who's puttin' you through hell is all you should have been thinkin' about. You've proved yourself right: you've won your chance to kill Chato.'

'I guess that is so,' Campbell replied. 'Though lying on that ledge listening to Mr Parker's screams I just couldn't convince myself of that.' Again Campbell's mind drifted away for a while before continuing with his story. 'Where I had gone over the edge of the butte wasn't a clear straight drop but rather a steep slope so I just kept on rolling until I was stopped abruptly by a clump of bush growing out of a fissure in the cliff face thirty or so feet down. The impact of hitting the brush flung me into the narrow slash in the rock. I lay there unseen by anyone looking down from the rim, half-mad, half-dead with pain, fearfully listening to Mr Parker's dying tortured screams as the murderous scum cut at him with their knives. Then I blacked out, coming to again in fading daylight.'

Campbell sighed deeply like a man who had had a heavy load taken from his shoulders. He raised his head and looked across the fire at Luke and Baldy. 'What happened next is only a vague recollection. I had to have a horse, water, and maybe a gun, in that order or die slowly of thirst on that ledge. And all those essentials to me staying alive were in the comanchero camp. Somehow I must have scrambled up the slope, and with the luck I never expected, I managed to get hold of a saddled horse, a canteen of water, but not wanting to stretch my luck by search-ing among the sleeping comancheros for a rifle or a pistol, I rein-walked the horse out of the silent camp. Then, mounted up and rode fast and wild like a man escaping from hell, as I surely was, Mr Culpepper.

'Existing on handouts from kind-hearted farmers and ranchers I finally made it to where you found me. That must have been nine months ago. Mr Pinkerton must think we are both dead, because I never contacted the agency of the failure of our assignment. Most of the time I was at the mine, I believed I was dead, spiritually, at least, Mr Culpepper.' He favoured Luke with a quizzical look. 'Is your reason for wanting to see Chato dead as pressing as mine, Mr Culpepper?'

'I'd like to think so, Mr MacColl,' replied Luke. 'One of Chato's wild boys put two arrows in me, and I ended by nearly drownin' in the Pecos. Though that ain't the main reason.' He told Campbell about the wagon-train massacre and how he felt obligated to hunt down Chato. 'It's the least I can do for lettin' those poor folks down.'

98

Campbell glanced across at Baldy. 'And your reason, Mr Springer,' he said, 'was it of account of your. . . ?'

'Because of my Injun haircut, Mr MacColl?' Baldy cut in. He grinned. 'Naw, that was just the doin' of an everyday bad-ass Injun. I kinda tagged along with Mr Culpepper after he got me out of a tight scrape with a bunch of cattle-lifters. I had nothing else particular to do in mind. Now we've bared our souls to each other, Mr Culpepper, and all of us agree that the world will be a better place if Chato was in Hell just how we gonna send him there? I figure it's time we come up with some sort of a plan.'

Luke gave him a lopsided grin. 'I've already thought of one, Mr Springer,' he said. 'I'll admit it ain't a humdinger of a plan, but I reckon it's the only option we've got. And it all depends on the co-operation of our young pard here.' Serious-faced, he looked at Campbell. 'Do you want to hear it, Mr MacColl? I won't be offended if you tell me you won't go along with it.'

'There's too much at stake for pards to get offended with each other, Mr Culpepper,' Campbell said. 'Tell me about your plan and what my role will be in it.'

'We make for Portales,' Luke began. 'And if it's OK with you, Mr MacColl, I'd like you to act as bait for the drawin' out in the open Chato's "eyes" in the town. Ask nosy questions again, as you did with your late pard. You might not need to ask around if the same fellas who jumped you are in Portales, they'll recognize you. This time it will be your pards who

99

will be doin' the cold-cockin'.' He grinned wolfishly. 'And I figure Mr Springer will know of some Injun way to persuade them to tell us where Chato's stronghold is.'

Baldy matched Luke's grin with a mirthless grimace of his own. 'A whole damn bagful of them, Mr Culpepper. If I really tried I would have an *hombre* tell me tales he wouldn't confess to a priest on his death bed.'

'It's a high risk I'm askin' you to take,' Luke said, turning to face Campbell again. 'I'm askin' you to put your life in the hands of a coupla old farts. But it's the only scheme I can come up with. I'm open to any other suggestions.'

Campbell felt a flicker of fear run through his body and hoped it hadn't shown in his face. He didn't want his partners to think he had weakened in his resolve to ride and fight alongside them, lost his self-respect and courage. He guessed he was still somewhat apprehensive about how he would bear up when his moment of truth finally came. He looked at his partners with a steady-eyed gaze. Although he had only known them for a few days they were tough men, men who would try their damnedest to protect him.

'I have to walk the line with you both sometime,' he said. 'Portales seems to be the obvious place to do it.' He smiled. 'This time I'll also have the Derringer handy.'

Both Luke and Baldy smiled. 'Good,' said Luke. 'Portales it is then. We ride in separate, from different directions, me and Baldy first. We'll all book in at the same roomin'-house then we've got you covered the twenty-four hours.' He got to his feet. 'Let's move out, pronto; I'm gettin' kinda uneasy bein' this close to Fort Sumner. It seems quiet enough now hereabouts but by what me and Mr Springer have been told there's a small war takin' place here. And wars, however small are trouble we want to stay well clear of. While we're in Portales you can go and see the town's doc, get that wound of yours checked over. Me and Mr MacColl ain't strong enough to stand the kick of that heavy gun of yours. And I'm bankin' on the Sharps bein' put to good use, blowing Chato all the way to Hell.'

Luke heard Baldy grunt; whether it was a grunt saying he was going to the doc, or not, he couldn't tell. Then he wondered why the hell he was talking to a man who had only stayed alive most of his life by being smarter than the wild redmen whose land he lived in. The old goat, Luke knew, would do what he thought he should do. He didn't need a nursemaid.

As the trio hit the trail to Portales, Campbell began to do some wondering of his own, wondering if Mr Culpepper and Mr Springer really meant to use their knives on any comanchero they managed to capture to make him talk. Or were his partners joshing him? Campbell's blood chilled slightly. He didn't think so. Smiling or not, Mr Springer would try out his bag of Indian tricks, as he put it.

Then his blood pumped warm again when he thought of the fearful agony that Mr Parker had suffered, not forgetting the pain and mental trauma Chato had put him through. The war against Chato

101

had to be fought by comanchero rules, no holds barred, or it was lost before they had fired the first shot. By thunder, Campbell thought, angrily, he would like to use the knife himself. Then he put all fanciful thoughts out of his mind and tried not to think too much of what could go wrong for them in Portales. Mr Culpepper had said it was a mad-ass plan. It was a sober-faced Campbell who rode the rest of the way to Portales.

ELEVEN

From the porch of the rooming-house, Luke watched Mr MacColl walk into the High Plains bar. The kid hadn't had a change of heart, lost his nerve; he was doing what had been asked of him. Now it was was up to him and Baldy to look out for the Pinkerton, or, like the German farmers and his former partner, Mr MacColl would end up dead.

Luke had ridden into Portales first, booking in at what Mr MacColl had told him was the only rooming-house in town. He had then come outside to sit on the porch to wait for his two *compadres* to show up.

Half an hour later, as the saloon lights were being lit, he saw Baldy coming out of the livery barn and make his way towards him, carrying his Sharps. Luke grinned, force of habit, he thought. Mr Springer's normal rooming-house would be anywhere beneath the big skies of Montana and Wyoming where a rifle was essential to a man sleeping peaceful as a fire and a blanket were. He had left his Winchester in the safe keeping of the livery-barn owner.

A while later, Baldy came out of the rooming-house, gave him a curt nod and strode across to the High Plains bar. Not long after, Campbell came into Portales. As he passed him on the porch, Luke said softly, 'Mr Springer's already across at the bar. We're ready when you are.'

Campbell quickly unpacked and was back outside on the porch within ten minutes. He managed to raise a confident smile at Luke. Now it was up to him. Knowing that his partners had every confidence in him helped to allay his fears somewhat. He stepped off the porch and walked boldly across to the bar.

Luke waited five or so minutes after the bar doors had swung closed behind Campbell before getting on to his feet. It was time for the hunt for Chato to be started in earnest. He eased his pistol in its holster; trouble could come fast and he wanted to meet it and come through on the winning side. He followed two trail-hands into the bar.

The bar was crowded with drinkers and card players, but he managed to find a seat at a table near the door and began to take in the scenery. From where he was sitting, Luke could see both of his partners, standing at the opposite ends of the long bar. Between them they had Mr MacColl well covered in the event of anyone making any hostile move against him.

Luke tensed up suddenly on noticing MacColl casting sidelong glances at three men playing cards at a table close by him. Two of the players were swarthy, hatchet-faced men, mixed-blood *hombres*,

Luke thought; the third, a big barn of a gringo, though he was as mean-faced as his *compadres*. Lying on the table was a long-barrelled shotgun, whose working parts were protected by a fringe-worked hide sleeve.

Campbell turned away from the bar and nodded in the direction of the three men. He couldn't see either of his partners but he knew they would be watching him. He wanted to let them know he believed he had spotted three comancheros, or at least men who traded with them.

Luke close-eyed the men. He noticed Baldy had changed his stance and was also looking at them. Had Campbell recognized them as comancheros? They looked vicious enough to be three of Chato's band of killers, but so did half the drinkers in the bar, including Mr Springer. Yet something about them had alerted Mr MacColl. It was time he got the kid out of the bar before the hard-cases cottoned on to the fact they were under surveillance, or recognized him as the Pinkerton agent who, they thought, had fallen to his death over the edge of a butte.

Luke stood up and, waiting until Mr MacColl had picked him out, did some head wagging of his own, jerking it in the direction of the door. Satisfied both of his partners had got the message he walked out of the saloon. He stood at the far end of the porch until Baldy, closely followed by Mr MacColl came out into the open, then stepped down into the side alley.

'Mr Culpepper,' Campbell said, as he came up to Luke, eager to tell him who he thought the three men were.

Luke raised a warning hand. 'Hold it a second, Mr MacColl,' he said. 'I want to make sure those *hombres* you were interested in ain't got likewise feelin's towards you. Both of you get further along the alley. I'll join you if everything's OK.' Baldy and Campbell waiting in the deeper darkness of the alley, pistols fisted, heard Luke say as came along the alley, 'It's OK. I reckon I was worryin' like some old maid. But it's better than bein' careless. We all know what grief and pain carelessness can bring on a man. Now, Mr MacColl, why were you so interested in those three hard-cases?'

'It was the gun lying on their table that first drew my attention, Mr Culpepper,' Campbell said.

'I saw it,' Baldy said. 'And a mighty fine piece it was.'

'Exactly, Mr Springer!' Campbell said excitedly. 'It was a Purdy, made by Purdy's of London, England, one of the finest gunsmiths in the world, a gun no ranch hand could afford to own. Even if he had the cash to buy one he would have to travel east as far as Chicago, m'be right back to New York to find a gun store that sold Purdys.'

'And you think that fine English gun was taken by the comancheros when they looted the camp of those Eastern dudes they massacred?' interrupted Luke.

'There's no other way, Mr Culpepper,' replied Campbell, 'that gun could have showed up here in Portales in the hands of those men.'

'I think we oughta have words with those *hombres*,' Baldy said. 'The white-eye will be the more loose-

106

mouthed under pressure. His two buddies have Injun blood in them. They'll take it as honour not to tell us anything no matter how uncomfortable we make it for them.'

Campbell suddenly felt a sickly feeling at the pit of his stomach. Torturing a man had suddenly lost its earlier appeal. As much as he wanted to see Chato dead, he could never take an active part in torturing a comanchero to have the satisfaction of avenging Mr Carter's death.

'It's a mite too soon to go out on the warpath, Mr Springer,' Luke said. 'Every bad-ass in the territory ain't a comanchero though their possession of that English gun needs explainin'.' Luke smiled icily. 'We won't find that out unless we step right up to the guys and accuse them outright of being comancheros.' Luke looked at Baldy. 'If they are, Mr Springer, we'll have to down those two Mexicans; we can't handle three prisoners.'

Campbell gulped hard, and got the chills again. Mr Culpepper was talking about cold-bloodedly killing men as though he was discussing the price of corn with Mr Springer. 'Is . . . isn't that acting as judge, jury and executioner, Mr Culpepper?' he said weakly.

'Out here, Mr MacColl,' Baldy said. 'Sometimes a man has to act like God, make up his own rules and act pretty damn quick on them if he wants to stay alive. If they are comancheros, then they're long past due for payin' the price for all their thievin' and killin'. Or would you let them live so they could sneak up on us along our back-trail? And remember,

107

the sonsuvbitches gave you no choice whether you lived or died.'

What Mr Springer had said was correct, Campbell knew, but still the action seemed drastic. Though he didn't openly say so to his partners.

Luke, sensing Campbell's uneasiness, said, 'Mr Springer's right, boy, we've got a whole passel of trouble somewhere ahead of us, we sure as hell don't want any comin' up behind us. I know some of our rough Western ways don't settle too easy on an Easterner's stomach, but that's the way things are played out here. And you've had to swallow some rough treatment.'

Luke smiled fatherly at Campbell. 'It ain't as though I'm goin' to back-shoot the pair. I'm givin' them the chance to draw. More than they gave the fellas they faced, I reckon.'

'Won't that be risky, Mr Culpepper?' Campbell asked in alarm. Though, he thought Mr Culpepper seemed to shrug off trouble with the ease a dog shakes water from its coat.

'Don't you fret none, Mr MacColl,' Luke replied. 'Mr Springer will be my back-up if things go wrong. And to tell you the truth, the chance those two fellas think they've got ain't no chance at all. They'll be sittin' there thinkin' thay can beat me to the draw when I'm standin' in front of them, bold-assed enough to still have my pistol holstered. What I—'

A smile of realization flooded across Campbell's face as he interrupted Luke. 'But you'll have my Derringer, won't you, Mr Culpepper?'

Luke beamed back at him. 'That I will, Mr

MacColl, that I will. Now I'd be obliged if you'd hand me that sneaky piece. I don't want its rig. Then me and Mr Springer can get back into the bar and keep a watchful eye on those three. You go and collect our gear from the rooming-house, saddle up our horses. Bring them here. Let me know when you come back, then I'll start the ball, OK?'

'OK, pard,' replied Campbell. He pulled up the sleeve of his jacket and slipped the Derringer out of its spring clip and handed it over to Luke. 'It's got two loads in and the safety's off, it's ready for instant use.'

Luke hefted the small gun in his hand. 'Two loads will be all I need, Mr MacColl. I'm not aimin' to start a shoot-out in a crowded saloon.' Luke turned and faced Baldy. 'It don't look as though you'll get to see the doc, Mr Springer. But I reckon a piddlin' little bullet hole won't put out an *hombre* who, stuck full of arrows, and carryin' his mule, walked sixty miles across rough country.'

'Yeah, you're right, Mr Culpepper,' Baldy said, equally straight-faced. 'We Big Horn country boys ain't noted for our delicate constitutions. As that fella I'm going to bend my Sharps' barrel over his head will soon find out.'

Luke was bellied up to the bar, trying not to make his eyeing of the three men too obvious. They would be natural suspicious-minded men, trigger-fingered, ready to leap to their feet and cut loose at all and everyone if they suspected they were being watched. Or quit playing cards and head outside to do some eyeing of their own. And for him to try and follow them would be asking to be shot down as soon as he stepped out of the bar.

Baldy was much closer to the table, keen, Luke opined, to put down the beefy gringo. He hoped the old goat wouldn't get carried away in the excitement and lay the man out grave cold. He gave Baldy a get-ready nod: he had seen Campbell come into the bar. The boy caught his eye then turned and walked back through the door. Luke smiled to himself. The boy wanted to be his back-up as well as Baldy when he confronted the three hard-cases, not to stay out in the street looking after the horses.

'The sounds of gunfire could spook them, Mr MacColl,' he had told him. 'While I'm only reckonin' that the Derringer's two loads will give me the upper hand things don't always pan out the way you hope. It could turn into a real shoot-out and scare the horses. And we'll not have the time to chase after them, or unhitch them from a post if we have to cut and run for it.' He didn't tell Campbell that if things didn't go right, he and Baldy would more than likely not make it alive to the door, let alone to their mounts. He hoped that situation wouldn't happen for then the kid would have to make a hard choice, stay and fight or hightail it out of Portales. Though Luke thought, knowing Mr MacColl's pride and loyalty to his partners, he would opt for standing his ground and making a fight of it. Luke cursed softly. Even when he was dead he could be responsible for someone's untimely death. Face set in hard, grim lines, he strode across the bar to the three men.

110

Baxter, the full-white, scowled up at Luke. Luke gazed at bleary, red-rimmed eyes. He had been hitting the bottle hard, he thought, which would be in their favour. A drunk would be easier to handle.

'What the hell are you standin' there for, mister?' Baxter mouthed, drunkenly.

Luke ignored him. Baldy would put paid to him when the time came. He kept his eyes on the expressionless-faced 'breeds, the men he had to kill when they made their play. He began to act out his bluff, all the while watching the 'breeds' shoulders for the giveaway twitching when they grabbed for their guns. He wouldn't be able to read their intentions in the dead-eyed faces.

'That fine gun lyin' there, *amigos*,' he said, 'once belonged to some dude hunters who got themselves massacred by a bunch of comancheros led by the renegade, Chato, not a coupla stones' throws away from here. I think you boys, and your fat-gutted gringo *compadre*, rode with those no-good killers and I'm takin' you in.'

Luke drew back his lips in a fierce grimace as he saw the warning movement of the 'breeds' shoulders. The bastards had fallen for his bluff, the killing time was here. Yet he waited that split-second until the 'breeds' guns were almost clear of the edge of the table before swinging the Derringer into view. He had to show clearly to any interested parties the 'breeds had drawn first.

The two shots showered ceiling dust on the alarmed drinkers flinging themselves to the floor or behind upturned tables and chairs for safety. The

111

two 'breeds bounced up against the backs of their chairs then flopped forwards across the table, each with a weeping red eye in their foreheads. Luke caught a glimpse of Baldy bringing down the Sharps hard on the third man's head, wincing at the sickening sound of steel striking against flesh and bone. Baldy's victim's expression changed from one of surprised shock at seeing his *compadres* gunned down to a fixed mask of pain as he slid from his chair, out to the wide, to hit the floor with a heavy thud.

'It's all over, folks!' Luke called out, turning away from the killing scene. 'I'm a US Marshal, and that gent with the rifle is my deputy!' he lied. 'These fellas we've had trouble with we believe they are comancheros, part of Chato's gang. I only wanted to ask them some questions but the 'breeds took it in their heads to make a fight of it!'

A beefy, longhorn-moustached man heaved himself up from beind a table and came across to Luke. Suspicious-eyed, he growled, 'A marshal, you say? I ain't seen you in the territory before and I reckon I'm acquainted with most of 'em. I'm Sheriff Hogan. I keep peace in this town and don't take kindly to any *hombre*, badge-totin' or not, havin' shoot-outs in a crowded bar.'

'I understand that, Sheriff,' replied Luke. 'But as I've said I only wanted to question these fellas and the next thing I knew the sonsuvbitches were pullin' guns on me.'

'Yeah, I saw that,' Sheriff Hogan said. 'They thought they had the edge on you.' He hard-eyed Luke. 'It was kinda fortunate you just happened to

112

be carryin' a hideaway gun, ain't it, Marshal?'

'Fortune had nothin' to do with it, Sheriff,' replied Luke. 'Ours is a hazardous profession, and it don't do not to take precautions for any upset. I got careless once, cost some folks their lives. My deputy relaxed his guard one time, Sheriff. Show them, Mr Springer.'

A smiling Baldy removed his hat. Luke heard one of the saloon girls give a muffled scream and a gasped, 'Holy Mother of God!' from the sheriff.

'I take your point, Marshal,' the sheriff said, though still out of sorts at having his poker game interrupted, especially when he was on a winning streak – and the loss of dignity to his calling by hiding like a scared kid behind a table with one of the girls. 'But,' he said, to regain his standing as the town's peace officer, 'it would have been only right and proper for you comin' into my town to make an arrest, to pay a call on me. Let me know what you're about. I could've let you have a coupla shotgun deputies; those 'breeds wouldn't have drawn on you then. Would've saved you havin' to kill them.'

'I didn't know they were in town, Sheriff,' Luke lied again. 'Me and my deputy only came into Portales for supplies. We walked into the bar for a drink, then I happened to see that gun there lyin' on the table and I knew the three must be comancheros, or have close links with them.'

Sheriff Hogan glanced down at the Purdy then favoured Luke with a puzzled look. 'It's only a shot-gun to me, a fancy one I'll admit, but what's it got to do with them bein' comancheros?'

113

'That "fancy" gun belonged to a party of Easterners out hereabouts on a huntin' trip,' Luke said. 'Chato and his comancheros massacred them, looted their camp. I wanted to ask them how the gun came to be in their possession, but the 'breeds weren't in the mood for talkin'. You saw the rest.'

'That's right, Sheriff,' Campbell said, as he came up to the pair. He had heard the two shots then silence. He knew it had been the Derringer that had been fired but he would be damned if he was going to stand out in the street holding horses' reins like some stable boy and wait until Mr Culpepper and Mr Springer came out of the bar and told him how things had gone down. He had loose-hitched the ropes round the post and stepped up on to the boardwalk and entered the bar.

'Who the hell's he?' Sheriff Hogan barked out. 'Another one of your deputies? He ain't gonna give the ladies a fright if he takes his hat off, is he?'

'I'm a Pinkerton agent, Sheriff,' Campbell said, stiffly. 'I take it you've heard of the agency.'

'Yeah, yeah, I've heard of them,' the sheriff replied, irritably. 'The whole territory was crawlin' with them a while back after the killin' of the dudes the marshal here spoke of. I heard two Pinkertons were killed by this Chato. Then a Mr Charles B. Nicholson, a well-heeled New Yorker, into steel and railroads, showed up, kickin' ass, army and lawmen, for not tryin' hard enough to rope in Señor Chato, the killer of his boy.' The sheriff looked down at the unconscious man. 'If he's a suspect comanchero I'd better put him behind bars until he comes round.'

114

He grinned at Luke. 'If he's one of the bastards who killed that big-shot's boy I might get me a medal.'

Campbell shot a glance at his two partners. They hadn't risked their lives to get a prisoner who could be their lead to Chato's stronghold, only to see him thrown in jail by a fat slob of a sheriff so he could get himself a piece of glory. He began to embellish the truth somewhat.

'The agency's motto, Sheriff, is, "We never sleep". Agents are still active in the territory working on the massacre case. I'm working closely with Marshal Culpepper. The marshal has been appointed specially by the Governor of New Mexico, who, incidentally, is a personal friend of Mr Charles B. Nicholson, to make every effort to track down Chato, the scourge of the state. We intended taking our prisoner to Fort Sumner where he will be interrogated by Mr Alan Pinkerton, the head of the agency, himself. That's how important that man is to us. Naturally, when I write my report, I'll mention that the Sheriff of Portales gave us every assistance regarding the apprehension of our suspect.'

Sheriff Hogan thought for a minute or two. Anything for a quiet life, he thought. He didn't want Pinkertons, Eastern big-shots or specially appointed state marshals descending on Portales. He couldn't cope with all the hassle. He would have to kiss goodbye to his regular poker game. The dude kid promised he would get a mention in his despatches. That ought to get him re-elected sheriff for another term.

'You can take that fella back to Fort Sumner, Mr

Pinkerton man,' he said. 'Hang the murderin' asshole when you've done talkin' to him.' He raised his voice and shouted, 'Billy Joe, Clancy, haul these two dead *hombres* along to the mortician's. One of you barkeeps clear away this table and bring out another, there's blood on this one! If you and your deputies are stayin' the night in town, Marshal,' the sheriff said to Luke, 'I'll lodge that fella you cold-cocked in a cell for the night. Kinda take him off your hands if you want a drink,' he grinned. 'Or female companionship.' The sheriff eyed the shot-gun longingly. 'M'be I oughta take charge of that gun as sort of evidence.'

'You do that, Sheriff,' replied Luke. The comancheros had had the gun once, if things went wrong for them he didn't want the sons-of-bitches to get their hands on it again. 'And thanks for the offer, but we're ready to ride out. There could be other comancheros in town who might try to effect a rescue of our prisoner, or silence him. He's the only lead to Chato we've got, I can't afford to take the chance of losin' him.'

'You could be right there, Marshal,' the sheriff admitted. 'That bastard Chato always seems one jump ahead of any posse tryin' to hunt him down. Bein' this is cattle country strangers regularly pass through Portales, some of them could be Chato's "eyes".'

Luke's smile held no warmth in it at all. 'If that *hombre* on the floor sings sweet and loud we'll be waiting at the spot Chato's aimin' to jump to.' He turned and faced Baldy. 'We'll tie him up good and

116

tight and sling him on the back of my horse, Mr Springer, then we'll head for Fort Sumner.'

Their ride to Fort Sumner was for the sheriff's benefit. Once clear of Portales they would head north where, Luke believed, Chato's stronghold lay. Then, at some lonely spot on the trail, Baldy would do his Indian tricks on their prisoner to find out exactly where Chato's camp was.

'Give me a hand, pards,' he said, and bending down, grabbed the inert comanchero by the shoulders.

TWELVE

At first light, Luke started the serious business of making their prisoner believe he would suffer the tortures of a hell on earth if he didn't show them the way to the comancheros' hold-out.

They had made camp in a hollow sheltered by a stand of close-growing cottonwoods, well clear of the main trail running between Portales and Fort Sumner. The campfire was low burning, Luke well aware there were all kinds of killing men prowling around the territory, Chato and his butchers, the factions in the so-called Lincoln County war, and the war band they had frightened off back along the trail. They were seen riding north and could be sitting around their own fire hereabouts.

Luke didn't want to face shooting trouble now. There was a good chance they would be able to sneak up on Chato's stronghold. Though sneaking up on the sonuvabitch's camp, Luke thought soberly, was a long ways from getting close enough to kill the comanchero chief, it was a move in the

119

right direction. It was up to Baldy and his knife to get them in closer.

'It's time we woke up that fella from his beauty sleep, Mr Springer,' he said. 'It looks as though you're ready to perform. You sure scare the hell outa me, and I reckon, Mr MacColl as well.

Baldy had stripped to his waist and removed his hat. His torso was as coppery as an Indian's, pock-marked with the white scars of old wounds, which made Luke think, what with being scalped and all, the old goat had suffered some painful experiences in his life. His story about walking all those miles in the high country stuck full of Sioux arrows could be almost true.

Baldy grinned. 'I'll do the wakin', Mr Culpepper,' he said. 'I ain't a purty sight, the sonuvabitch will think Judgement Day has arrived, scare him real good straight off.' He spat on the blade of the Bowie he held in his right hand, heard it sizzle and evapo-rate instantly in a slight puff of steam. His grin became demonic.

Campbell shuddered, hearing Mr Carter's agoniz-ing screams again. Mr Culpepper was right, Mr Springer's appearance frightened him. With that fearful head scar and body wound marks, he would not look out of place standing alongside that arch-fiend, Chato. Though he told himself that Mr Springer was only play-acting, Campbell gave both his partners a long, searching look and came up with the uneasy feeling neither of them *were* acting. In fact, Mr Springer seemed eager to use his knife on their prisoner. He asked himself the question of

120

does the means justify the end? And found he could-n't answer it. One thing he did know for certain, he was too queasy inside to stay and watch what was about to be done to the comanchero. He prayed it was only play-acting.

'I'll check on the horses, Mr Culpepper,' he said. 'That's if you don't need me here.'

'You do that, Mr MacColl,' Luke replied. 'That *hombre* won't be no problem to me and Mr Springer.' He guessed why the kid couldn't stay and didn't blame him. Baldy could be forced to draw some of his blood, painfully, to give him the impression he was in the hands of killing men as merciless as any comanchero. Like Mr MacColl, Luke wasn't anxious for that to happen, but his mind went back to the sight of the rough wooden markers on the graves along the Pecos and he convinced himself that dras-tic measures had to be taken to prevent similar such-like massacres of innocent folk.

Baxter groaned loudly and came alive, slowly and painfully. His head was still pounding from the vicious blow he had taken and his right cheek stiff with caked blood from the wound. And he discov-ered he was bound hand and foot and tied to a tree. At least the bastards who had taken him hadn't shot him like they had Felix and Jose and he wondered why. They couldn't be lawmen, or he would have been behind bars not feeling all cramped to hell with being roped to a tree for most of the night. Who his captors were had him worried.

Then, through pain-blurred eyes, he saw a bald-headed old man dressed only in buckskin pants, a

121

knife glinting ominously in his hand, coming towards him and he really began to worry. Baxter blurted out a stream of panic-stricken curses. Since being knocked out in the bar by white men, Indians had somehow got their hands on him. What they intended doing to him almost made him lose control of his bladder. Felix and Jose had been the lucky ones, he thought, wildly.

As the knife-wielding bronco came closer, Baxter gasped in surprise. He was a white man and he wasn't bald but had been scalped. But the ugly, mad-eyed face belonged to an Indian worked up into the killing lust. Baxter lost the battle with his bladder.

It might not be such a blood-letting job after all, Luke thought, the comanchero hadn't wet his pants with joy. He gazed down at him. 'Mister,' he grated, 'we know you and the two 'breeds I shot back there in Portales rode with Chato and his gang, that shot-gun told us that. Now I ain't bothered if you were in the murderous bunch who killed the Eastern hunters and stole their fancy guns and gear, all I want to know is where Chato's hole-up is. Give me that information, pronto-like, and you'll be free to go. But only in the direction I point you in.' Luke grinned an all-tooth grim smile. 'I can't have you ass-kickin' it back to your boss and telling him that some *hombres* are comin' in to kill him.'

A nerve-twitching-faced Baxter looked up at his captor. He saw nothing in the tall, horse-faced son-of-a-bitch's frozen-eyed gaze that gave him any comfort. 'You can't let that old man use his knife on me, mister!' he pleaded, throat dry with fear. 'It . . .

it ain't Christian for a white man to carve up another white man!'

Baldy laughed. 'Do you hear that, Mr Culpepper? He's talkin' there about Christians. And I bet the murderin' sonuvabitch has bein' doin' the Devil's work since he could cock a pistol. He sure ain't been handing the Bibles out when he rode with the comancheros.' He knelt down and ripped open their prisoner's shirt and laid the knife close to his chest. Scowling, he snarled, 'Now quit stallin' and tell my pard what he wants to know, or so help me I'll start cuttin'!'

Baxter's eyes widened with terror. He gave a deep hiss of pain and drew back hard against the tree as he felt the heat of the blade and smelt the acrid stench of his singed chest hair. Yet, stubbornly, he refused to talk. He was hanging on to the desperate hope his captors were bluffing against the sure certainty that Chato would see he died real hard and painful if he found out he had betrayed him.

Baldy raised the stakes in the bluffing game by slashing the knife across the comanchero's chest, a trickling red line following the point of the blade.

Campbell, making himself busy at the horse lines, heard the shrill scream. He listened, nerves twanging painfully, but heard no more tortured cries. He prayed it wasn't because Mr Springer had been too heavy-handed with his knife and killed their prisoner. There and then he decided, if he was alive after all this was over, and still a Pinkerton agent, he would cry off taking any assignment west of the Mississippi. The brutal, cold-blooded way justice was administered out here, west of the Pecos, turned his stomach; he wanted no part of it.

Baxter broke. 'I'll talk, I'll talk!' the words bubbling out as hysterically as his scream. 'Just don't let that white-Injun work on me with his knife any more!'

Luke breathed a silent gasp of relief. Baldy's play-acting – he hoped it was just that – had scared the wits out of their prisoner.

'There, Mr Springer,' he said. 'I know you'll be a mite disappointed at not sheddin' any more of this *hombre*'s blood but I told you he would soon see reason when he knew we meant business and tell us want we want to know.' Luke cold-smiled down at their captive. 'But don't put your big knife away just yet in case this *hombre* is tryin' to play us along. If he is, you can show him what real pain is.'

Baldy stood up, still wearing his mad-eyed scowl. 'If the sonuvabitch is stallin', Mr Culpepper, then you won't be able to stop me from slicin' him up. I've kinda worked myself up for some blood-lettin'. Ain't done any since I left the high plains.'

Baxter looked up in horror at Baldy. He knew the painful manner of death Chato would give him if he found out he had betrayed him, but that possible death was forty miles away. An equally agonizing death was only inches from his nose, in the hands of a man as blood-mad as Chato.

'Chato's camp is forty miles north-west of here,' he said. 'Cut through those mountains you can see, until you come across a crick. Follow it due east until you come across two pointed peaks and you'll

124

be almost at the camp.' Baxter didn't tell his captor that Chato had double guards posted on four lookout posts, day and night, on the last half-mile of the trail into the camp. The three bastards would be dead a long ways before they reached the camp.

Luke saw the light of that hopeful thought in the comanchero's eyes. He grinned. 'We ain't so foolish as to ride right up to the stronghold's front door. When we go in we'll go in Injun-style, quietly and quickly. Isn't that so, Mr Springer?' Baldy beamed at Baxter. Which to the comanchero, losing his last ray of hope that his pain and the killing of Felix and Jose would be avenged, seemed as frightening as the old bastard's scowl.

'Is Chato at the camp now?' Luke asked. Baldy waved his knife in front of Baxter's face and made to go down on his knees alongside him. 'Take it easy, Mr Springer,' Luke said. 'Give the *hombre* time to answer. He's been co-operative up till now. He knows how painful it will be if he turns awkward.'

'Yeah, he's there,' Baxter said. And to show how co-operative he was being, he added, 'Though he'll be ridin' out tomorrow, south, to the Rio Grande to meet up with a Comanche chief. And that's all I can tell you!'

'OK, OK,' Luke said. 'I believe you. Now that just leaves us with the problem of what to do with you, friend.'

'But you promised I'd go free if I told you what you wanted!' Baxter cried. 'I had nothin' to do with the killing of those dude hunters! The two Mexes you shot in Portales were in on the raid, that's how they came by that shotgun!'

Before he could answer the comanchero, Luke heard Baldy gasp, 'Where the hell did they come from!' He turned and saw five riders picking their way through the trees.

'Not by the way we come into the timber,' replied Luke, eyes narrowing in concern. 'But it's too late to do anything about it. They ain't some of Chato's bunch, or they would have come in shootin', but if they favour one side or the other in the Lincoln County trouble it would be advisable not to go for our guns, or they could take it that we support the opposite faction. I only hope Mr MacColl is OK.'

'They're only kids, Mr Culpepper,' Baldy said in surprise.

'That may be true,' Luke said. 'But they're armed up and as tetchy-lookin' as growed-up *pistoleros*. We'll have to try and sweet-talk our way out of any trouble those kids are bringin' in with them, Mr Springer.'

Campbell saw the riders enter the timber and dropped flat to the ground, trusting that the horses' legs would shield him from the riders who rode past the horse line and right up to the camp. He had just decided to go back to the camp to see how the prisoner was faring. Mr Culpepper and Mr Springer's attitudes to law-enforcing could never be his way, but they were his partners and he had to stand by them. And that standing by them was here right now; his partners could be in danger. He put aside all his worrying thoughts about how law and order issues were dealt with west of the Pecos and reached up and drew out Mr Springer's shotgun from the pack on Jethro's saddle and began belly-crawling towards the camp.

Baxter's face lit up in a hopeful smile when he saw the riders. 'Billy!' he yelled. 'These bastards have took me prisoner! They're workin' on me with a knife like some heathen Injuns!'

Billy the Kid leaned forward in his saddle, elbows resting on the saddle horn and cast a curious glance at the two 'white' Indians. He wasn't someone who was easily rattled but the two men unsettled him somewhat. They were men who wouldn't be intimidated by his reputation in the territory, if they knew who he was. Press them into a corner, Billy thought, and the old man with the Indian haircut would leap at him and slice him open with that big pig-sticker he was toting, even if he emptied his Colt into him. As for his pard, he had the unwavering, all-seeing look of Marshal Pat Garrett. The tall man was a lawman, or at one time wore a peace-officer's badge. Prod him and he would get trouble.

Marshal Garrett was the reason he and his boys were making for the dog-dirt town of Portales. Garrett and his shoot-on-sight posse were making things too hot for him across at Fort Sumner, pressing him hard enough to force them to stay clear of the main trail to Portales and skulk along dry washes and gullies like hunted game. Otherwise they wouldn't have spotted the camp and came to see who was at the fire. And here they were, Billy opined, out of Pat Garrett's skillet and into two hard-faced *hombres*' fire – if he pushed the bastards to a showdown. The flames of that fire suddenly licked around Billy's ass as he heard the ominous clicks of the hammers of a shotgun being drawn back. Billy cursed softly and stayed resting forward on his saddle.

'We're not seeking any trouble, mister,' Campbell said, voice hard and steadier than he was feeling. 'I take it you men are actively engaged in the war we have heard is going on in the county. Well, we have no part in that conflict. Our war is with Chato and his comancheros. But if you think otherwise I'll tell you this, though it goes against my principles; if you make a hostile move against my partners, I'll back-shoot with this shotgun. And at this range at least three of you will cease worrying how things are going for your side in the war.'

Billy laughed and straightened up in his saddle. 'You're makin' war against Chato? Do you hear that, Charlie?' he said to the rider alongside him. 'We`ve rode into the camp of three loco *hombres*. Goin' up against Chato without a company of blue-belly horse soldiers to back you up is one of the fastest ways I know for a *hombre* to get himself dead. I hope you gents don't take it unkindly me tellin' you that. You with the scattergun at my back, you'll get no trouble from me and my boys. You and your pards' plates are heaped with it already, though it ain't hit you yet. Are you lawmen?' a curious Billy asked.

'Vigilantes, you could say, Billy,' Luke said. 'The three of us all have damn good reasons for seeing Chato dead. Kinda blood-for-blood situation.' He fish-eyed Billy. 'It sure upsets me to hear that gringos are killin' each other hereabouts for what reason I

128

don't know, or care about while Chato and his rene-
gades are runnin' free, butcherin' New Mexican
women and children. It seems that the so-called
hombres in the territory ain't got any pressin' intention of tryin' to rope in Chato.'

'Or ain't got the balls, Mr Culpepper,' Baldy said,
fierce-eyeing the riders.

'Me and my boys have balls, old man!' Billy said
angrily. 'But we've prices on our heads and when
lawmen like Marshal Pat Garrett are trailin' us, we
need all the time we've got to look out for ourselves.
And besides, Chato and his bunch are hard *hombres*
to track down. We don't even know where the
sonuvabitch rests up!'

'We know where that is, Billy,' Luke said. He
jerked a thumb at his prisoner. 'That feller is a
comanchero. My pard kinda persuaded him to tell
us where Chato's camp is.'

'Comanchero, eh?' Billy said. The look he gave
Baxter told the comanchero his plea for help had
fallen on deaf ears, and chilled his blood. Billy the
Kid had given him the killing look. 'So you know
where Chato's camp is,' the Kid continued. He
favoured Luke with a mocking buck-toothed grin.
'What are you gonna do, surround it?'

'What we're after,' Luke said calmly, holding on to
his temper, 'is to get near enough to the stronghold
for Mr Springer to draw a bead on Chato. We know
what the bastard looks like. Mr MacColl, who's the
gent holdin' the shotgun on you, was Chato's prisoner once. We ain't contemplatin' a stand-up fight
with Chato's outfit; all we want is a few seconds of

good luck that places Chato, in the back sights of Mr Springer's Sharps, then we hightail it out of there.'

Luke was wishing Billy would do likewise out of their camp. Though Billy had said he wasn't about to cause trouble, wild kids with prices on their heads were unstable characters. And Billy, Luke figured, was a youth of wildly swinging moods: laughing and joking with you one minute then still grinning his toothy smile, capable of gunning you down.

'You can come round front, Mr MacColl,' he said. 'We'll take Billy at his word that he's payin' us a friendly call.' Billy didn't think much of Mr Culpepper's plan to put paid to Chato, less so when Mr MacColl came into view and joined his partners. MacColl had spoken like some high-faluting Yankee lawyer and, when he saw him, Billy knew for certain he was an Eastern dude, not much older than he was. Billy thought he could be lookin' at his grand-pappy, pa and elder brother. Mr Culpepper spoke of a few minutes of good luck. In his considered opinion, the three loco *hombres* would need a year's good luck to get anywhere near Chato unseen, let alone kill him.

He told Luke about some of his misgivings about his plan. 'You might not be able to make a run for it, Mr Culpepper,' he said. 'Those comancheros will know their own backyard real well. They'll jump you before you get clear.'

'Chato bein' dead could kinda throw the rest of the comancheros off balance,' Luke said. 'They could want to elect a new leader before doin' anything about the killin' of their old one, like the

130

Injuns do. I grant you it ain't much of a plan, in fact it ain't no plan at all. But we've got ourselves a long ways closer to Chato than when we first started out and if our luck stays with us there's nothin' to stop us from finishin' things in our favour.'

Billy grunted. Crazy or not he had to admire men who were about to ride calmly along a suicide trail. He thought it must be one big hate the trio held against Chato, to want to carry out such a mad-assed plan.

Then Billy had a disturbed feeling: was it because he was upset at being called ball-less? Or was he having pangs of jealousy knowing how high the three *hombres*' rep would be if they succeeded in killing Chato? Out-shining his and his boys standing in the territory; the kids who were running Marshal Pat T. Garrett ragged; who came and went when they pleased, shooting their way out of trouble. Why, the Mexicans sang songs in their cantinas about the wild exploits of Billy the Kid. Even Governor Lew Wallace had offered him a free pardon if he gave himself up peacefully.

Then, surprising himself, he said, 'Boys, what say you if we tag along with these three gents, and if things seem favourable, help them to kill Chato? It'll be a mite more excitin' than sittin' on our asses in some stinkin' bordello in Portales all screwed up in case Garrett and his deputies come poundin' along Main Street to shoot us down like mad dogs.' Billy grinned. 'That's if Mr Culpepper and his pards don't mind ridin' alongside a bunch of desperadoes wanted by the law.'

131

Charlie Bowdrie, Billy's right-hand man, knew it would be a waste of time trying to talk Billy out of what he thought was the most hare-brained caper the Kid had ever come up with, because he didn't like his schemes criticised. Though this time he felt worried enough, and bold enough, to state his doubts about Billy's suggestion.

'There's a helluva lot more of them comancheros than us, Billy,' he said. 'And if we're lucky to kill Chato, I can't see Marshal Pat Garrett handin' us the re-ward money. The only thing that long streak of misery will dish out to us is a magazine-load of Winchester shells.'

Billy laughed. 'You worry too much, Charlie. As I said, if we don't like the situation when we get to Chato's hole-up why we just swing round and head for Portales. It ain't like we're soldier boys, and Mr Culpepper ain't our capt'n, orderin' us to do this and that.' He looked at Luke. 'Are you willin' to allow me and my boys to ride with you, Mr Culpepper?'

Luke had already thought he was willing to accept the Devil's help, if the Devil carried a gun, to kill Chato. While Old Nick had not yet volunteered his services, he was being offered help from men who, he had a gut-feeling, would be meeting up with the Devil before they got much older.

'I have no problem with that, Billy,' he said. 'Neither will my pards. As I said, killin' Chato is all we're interested in. Though I ain't a blue-belly capt'n, I must insist from now on in, Mr Springer will tell us how we ought to do things. We're within

132

forty miles of Chato's stronghold and we don't want to ride there like a bunch of war-time Missouri brush boys raidin' some Kansas free-stater's holdin'. We go in Injun-style, a style Mr Springer has picked up by livin' among the Sioux and the Crow way up in Montana.'

Billy almost told Mr Culpepper that his old pard couldn't have been much of an Indian fighter to allow an Indian to sneak up on him and lift his hair, but to keep friendly with his new partners, he said, 'Me and my boys can move around sneaky-like, Mr Culpepper.' Then looking at the prisoner, he said, 'What about him? He's a comanchero, isn't he, a woman and child killer?' Billy's hand blurred in movement and the Colt it held barked and flamed. Baxter slumped in his bonds, a red stain spreading across his shirt front. The pistol was slipped deftly back into its holster and a smile was back on Billy's face. 'That's one less comanchero we've got to kill, Mr Culpepper. Now we're ready to ride out on your sayso.'

The shooting had happened so fast and unexpectedly that Luke had had no time to explain to Billy he was going to let the comanchero free for being forthcoming with the whereabouts of Chato's camp. And his early reading of Billy riding along the turnpike to Hell had been proved justified. Then, he thought, coldly, siccing killers on to killers seemed good tactics.

The cold-blooded killing had only confirmed Campbell's strongly held belief that God had no part in creating some of the men west of the Pecos.

133

Though Baldy saw the stark logic of Billy's action, that of never leaving a live enemy behind you, he made a mental note to keep a watchful eye on the young killer. He had seen by the look on Billy's face he was of a rare breed, someone who enjoyed killing. He could get the urge to kill his three new partners.

'We'll break camp right away, Billy,' Luke said. 'We need to check out the approaches to Chato's camp before dark. Then we've got all night to try and come up with some sort of a war plan. I'd be obliged if you ride point, Mr Springer, warn us if we're makin' dust, we don't want to make a hash of it now. Does that sit with you OK, Billy?'

'It's your show, Mr Culpepper,' Billy replied. His kid's grin lit up his face again. 'I'll tell you when it ain't. Now, if you allow my boys to step down we'll finish off that coffee you've got heatin' on the fire while you get packed up.'

THIRTEEN

Baldy hadn't let them down, Luke thought. He had led them to the hills unseen, as far as could make out, and fast. Knowing that Chato was riding south tomorrow, time wasn't on their side. He noticed that even Billy was impressed by the old mountain-man's skill on the trail.

When they reached the creek their prisoner had told them to follow, Baldy suddenly drew up Jethro and began gazing hard at the high ridges ahead of them.

'Mr Culpepper,' he said sharply, 'I think it's advisable to go to ground in yonder rockfall.'

'The old man ain't gettin' nervous, is he, Mr Culpepper?' Billy said. 'Now we're gettin' close to Chato's stronghold? I reckon what with bein' tailed by lawman and bounty hunters, I've got me a fine instinct for sensin' trouble comin' my way and it ain't sendin' me any alarm signals right now,'

Luke grinned. 'Me neither, Billy. But Jethro, Mr Springer's mule can smell comancheros, or the part-Injuns who run with Chato, hereabouts. See the mule's ears stickin' up? That's a warnin' sign.'

135

Billy's eyes widened in disbelief. 'You're ribbin' me, ain't you, Mr Culpepper?'

'Billy,' Luke said, as he swung down from his mount, 'if you want to stay alive you'd better believe it. That mule don't kid. Make for those rocks as Mr Springer says.'

'OK, boys,' Billy said, albeit reluctantly, still doubting Luke's word. 'Do the old man's biddin'. But if any one of you tells any *hombre* we took orders from a dumb-ass mule, so help me I'll plug him.'

Once sheltered by the rocks, Baldy explained to Luke what his next moves were. 'I'll scout ahead on foot,' he said. He grinned at Billy. 'As Jethro's told us, there's comancheros close by. That prisoner of ours didn't tell us Chato had lookouts posted in these canyons; he was hopin' we'd walk slap bang into them.'

When Baldy was ready to move out, he was stripped to the waist and had marked his face, Indian-style, with moistened dirt and was only armed with his Bowie. With a curt nod to Luke, he slipped out between the rocks and was gone from their view in a matter of minutes.

'He's more Injun than a real bronco,' Billy said. 'I don't scare easily, but I wouldn't care to meet up with the old goat in the dark, especially when he's heftin' that big-bladed knife.'

'That's what he's doin', Billy,' replied Luke. 'Actin' like an Injun. If he's unlucky enough to get captured or killed by the comancheros, what with bein' scalped and all, they'll take him for a lone crazy white man. Not one of a band of men comin' in to raid them.'

Luke was having second thoughts about taking Billy and his gang as allies. His plan for seeing Chato dead was for Baldy to be perched on some rock high above the camp, with MacColl, using his army glasses to point Chato out to Baldy. Then it was all up to the old man and his Sharps. Afterwards they'd pull out fast. Billy, he opined wouldn't want to sit on his ass when lead was flying around; he'd want to take part in the action. And they weren't strong enough to have a shoot-out with a whole gang of killers, and pull through.

Luke began to worry; Baldy had been out almost three hours and it was coming on dark. He had heard no sounds of gunfire so unless Baldy had been killed silently, he assumed he was still alive. He heard Jethro whinny and stamp his feet. Luke smiled his relief: Baldy was on his way in.

Billy was half asleep up against a rock, wishing he had taken his boys to Portales after all; this waiting was boring the pants off him. Suddenly, in front of his nose a dirt-painted face appeared as from out of nowhere. Billy jerked upright. 'Jesus!' he gasped 'You almost scared the crap outa me, old man!'

Baldy grinned. 'If I'd been a real bronco, Billy, I would have had your hair hangin' on my belt. Which would have been a shame because you and your boys are goin' to get all the shootin' you can handle. Come across with me to Mr Culpepper and I'll explain how I think we could not only put paid to Chato, but most of his murderous bunch.'

The killing ground was a bluff overlooking the

137

comancheros' camp, Baldy told them. Loose soil and shale for the first hundred feet or so, then levelling off halfway up into a rocky and brush-covered strip of ground, then climbing again to the ridge peak. 'I'll be up on the top ridge,' Baldy said. 'And start needlin' the sonsuvbitches with the Sharps. When they see it's only one man with a single-shot rifle who's puttin' them down for good they'll come up that bluff seekin' my blood. They'll have to use both hands to haul themselves up that first stretch of the bluff so they'll not have their guns drawn.' Baldy favoured them all with a fierce bronco-grin. 'When they make it to the ledge, you gents, hunkered down in the brush, will be able to shoot them down as slick as the Sioux wiped out Custer's command way up there on the Rosebud. Then I reckon eight Winchesters, rapid firin', should send the comancheros left down below in the camp harin' for safer holes.'

It seemed a better plan than his, Luke thought, though he did raise a point. 'What about Chato?' he asked Baldy. 'Do you want Mr MacColl up there with you on the ridge to point him out?'

'Naw,' Baldy replied. 'I'm firin' at buffalo-gun range. Mr MacColl will serve our cause better by being with you bushwhackers.'

The plan seemed mad-assed enough to please Billy. He was always willing to take a chance if it was exciting enough, and if shooting came into it. Though he did ask Baldy how he knew so much about the lie of the land at the stronghold. Good-naturedly he said, 'Did you walk bold-assed right into the camp, Mr Springer? And ask them where the best spot was for a fella to shoot down on them?'

'Something like that, Billy,' Baldy said, matching Billy's humour. 'Why, one of them offered me some coffee and beans, but I had to decline, tellin' him I had to get back and put some youngsters to bed. And that will be only for a coupla hours 'til the moon gets up. Then you're all goin' to sweat your balls off doin' some hard climbin'.'

FOURTEEN

Chato was in a good mood. He was sitting in a battered old hide armchair at one of the campfires, drawing contentedly on a fine gringo cigar. Felix, one of his lieutenants, had sent word back from Portales that the army patrols searching the territory for him were now far west of Fort Sumner. That information meant he would have a clear run south to the border with his band for a rendezvous with the Comanche chief, White Eagle.

It would be a good trade, Chato opined. He had much to offer White Eagle, guns, ammunition, whiskey and white women. Chato's lips curled in the shadow of what passed for a smile on the all-bone face. Maybe not virgins, he had seen to that, but strongly built women, able to work hard for the chief and provide enjoyment for him at night on his blanket. White Eagle would trade horses and cattle in exchange. Felix and Jose, and the gringo, Baxter, were due back before noon and as soon as they rode in he would give the order to ride for the Rio Grande.

A sour-faced Howling Wolf, wrapped up in his blanket, at a nearby fire, gazed angrily into the flames. He wished he had the 'breed, Chato, dangling on the end of a rope over them, savouring the pleasure of his screams as his flesh began to roast. His grand dreams of riding out of Chato's camp with twenty or so Winchester repeating rifles and belts of shells, enabling him to double the strength of his band, had come to naught. The guns Chato had traded with him for the Mexican gold were old, single-shot rifles, some with worn-out barrels and broken stocks. The 'breed had made him lose face as a chief in front of his warriors. 'Warriors'. Howling Wolf spat in the fire. He had allowed his men to have several bottles of whiskey so they could forget their disappointment at not being the proud owners of repeating rifles. Now they were sprawled out in a drunken stupor, the unblooded boys lying in their own vomit.

The hatred he felt for Chato burned like a flaming brand in Howling Wolf's chest. Somehow, he promised himself, he would have to kill the comanchero dog or he would never get any peace of mind in this life or the life he was destined to live when his time came to pass through the gateway of death.

Luke, crouched low in the brush, alongside Campbell and Charlie Bowdrie, waited impatiently for Baldy to start the small war. He opined the old man was waiting for the last of the night mist to clear away from the camp before he opened up with the Sharps. The camp was waking up, men relieving themselves, women building up the fires ready for cooking meals. Luke wanted to catch the comancheros still half asleep, with their pants more or less down. It had been a hazardous trail from the lonely graves on the Pecos, and now his moment of truth was only the sound of a rifle shot away. Luke thought that Billy and the rest of his boys, in the brush on the other side of the track the comancheros would have to follow to get to Baldy, were feeling just as edgy.

Billy also wanted the action to start, to make someone pay for his aching feet. The old man had led them up hills, down into canyons and draws until he didn't know if he was still in New Mexico or the Texas Panhandle. He wasn't quite sure whether Mr Springer had Indian blood in him but he was certain he was part goat. He had brought them down into the brush without pausing for a rest or to wonder in which direction he should head, then hauled himself back up the ridge they had just come down from. Billy hoped the old goat hadn't tired himself out and fallen asleep up there, or by hell he'd stroll down into that camp and start the war himself.

Baldy laid the Sharps' sights on a comanchero standing at one of the fires. He had seen no signs of a man wearing a fancy-looking Mexican officer's tunic that young MacColl told him Chato rigged himself out in. Once he started the killing, the sly murdering son-of-a-bitch whould soon show himself; then by hell, Baldy thought, he would be dead. He pulled the trigger and the Sharps kicked and barked flame and smoke.

Howling Wolf saw a comanchero flung backwards from a fire, arms grabbing wildly at the air, and fall to the ground, dead as any man he had seen killed. Then he heard the resounding crack of the gun that had fired the deadly shot. It was the gun that killed from great distances, the weapon of the old white-eye who had warned him with the same gun not to attack him and his *compadre*. The two white-eyes, he thought must hold great hatred for Chato and have the fearless courage of Cheyenne dog soldiers to attack so many of their enemies.

Howling Wolf sprang to his feet as another comanchero fell victim to the long gun, and began poking his men in the ribs with his rifle to rouse them out of their drunken sleep. It was time they rode out of the camp before they got shot. He owed no loyalty to Chato to fight alongside him, and he was beholden to the old white-eye for not killing him on their first meeting. And while the comancheros were busy fighting their battle he would help himself to some of the repeating rifles that were in crates on a wagon near where their horses were tethered.

It was as though he was shooting into a herd of buffalo to Baldy, targets that he couldn't miss. Methodically, every five or six seconds he sent a comanchero on his road to hell. Turning the once quiet camp into an uproar of shouting and cursing men, running every which way to seek shelter from the deadly fire. Added to the noise, were the screams and cries of the terrified women and children.

Chato brought some order into the chaos raging

all around him. The sound of the first shot had him leaping out of his chair, his cigar dropping from a mouth open wide in alarm. He dived for cover behind the nearest wagon and began, frantically, to take stock of the situation that had suddenly burst upon him. It wasn't long before he realized it wasn't a full-scale attack on the camp by US cavalry. He started dirty-mouthing. one lone gunman was killing his men. He stood up and ran across to the nearest bunch of his men who were firing their rifles at the sniper on the ridge behind a barricade of crates.

'You loco bastards!' he screamed, waving his pistol at them. 'The sonuvabitch is out of range! We've got to go up there and take him! And take him alive so we can kill him slowly!'

By curses and threats to shoot them if they didn't follow him, Chato rallied about a dozen of his men, then they set off in a crouching low, zigzag run for the bluff. Baldy hadn't intended on firing on them, his whole plan was to draw the comancheros on to him, and into the ambush until he saw one of the leading comancheros wore an officer's tunic. Baldy smiled. He didn't think God answered old sinners' prayers. He thumbed a load into the Sharps and drew a bead on the comanchero chief.

A comanchero slightly ahead of Chato slipped sideways on a patch of loose shale and caught the shot that was meant for Chato. His head blew apart in a bloody mess of bone and brains. His body fell against Chato's, knocking him to his knees. He fell flat on his face and slid down to the bottom of the bluff.

Which suited Chato well. It had not been a good idea being up front with his men wearing his *federale* officer's tunic. He knew the shot had been meant for him and the sniper wasn't going to have another chance to shoot off his head. Bruised and bleeding, Chato began belly crawling along the foot of the bluff, seeking a hole to lie up in until his men brought down the sniper, every few yards casting a fearful glance upwards to make sure he was out of sight of the killing gun.

Baldy swore. He had had Chato in his sights and missed the son-of-a-bitch. He took a quick glance down but got no sighting of him so he looked for a new target.

'Get ready, Mr MacColl,' Luke said softly. 'They're here!'

Campbell saw a ragged line of comancheros come into view then bunch up to make it through the brush. Several of them began to unsling their rifles from their shoulders, or draw their pistols. It was Billy who opened up the killing time, firing non-stop from the hip with his rifle. Then a deadly hail of Winchester shells from both clumps of brush swept the comancheros off their feet as though blown down by a high wind. Some lay where they fell, others tumbled back down the bluff setting the whole of the loose face moving. The few comancheros who had been following them turned and took off in a sliding, jumping run to escape the wall of rocks thundering down on them, and kept on running once they had reached the flat in the desperate haste of men who knew they had lost the day.

A Rebel-yelling Billy came out of the brush, his smile reaching his ears when he saw the comancheros fleeing for the horse lines. When Luke and the rest of the bushwhackers joined him, he said, excitedly, 'We whupped them, Mr Culpepper. We whupped them good!'

'That we did, Billy,' replied Luke. 'You can put your guns down, *amigos*, we've done enough killin' this day. We'll go down now and tell the womenfolk the fight's over and they can tend to their wounded. Mr MacColl can check over the bodies to see if Chato's body's among them. Is that OK, boy?'

'OK, Mr Culpepper,' Campbell replied. Though he didn't relish turning over dead bodies to see if one of them was Chato's. He had read about massacres in his history books at school, but never in his wildest dreams had he thought he would be taking an active part in one. He felt blood drained.

The sudden burst of rifle fire changed Howling Wolf's plans of getting hold of the new rifles. It was a good killing-day for the old white-eye and his *compadres*; he didn't want himself and his band added to that total. While the old man may have saved his life, he could expect no mercy from the men with the rifles. All Indians off the agency were shot down like mad dogs. He shouted at his men to pick up the rifles of the dead comancheros, but to be quick if they wanted to live.

Then the Great Spirit smiled on Howling Wolf, or so he thought, when he saw Chato hiding behind a close-by hut. Chato only realized the danger he was in when he felt a split-second of blinding pain as

147

Howling Wolf's rifle butt struck him hard on the head, then everything went black for him. Part-carrying, part-dragging, Howling Wolf got the unconscious Chato to the horses and slung him across the back of a saddled beast. Leaping on to his own pony he led his warriors out of the camp in a dust-raising gallop.

Baldy had joined them when Campbell came back to report to Luke that Chato's body wasn't among the dead or wounded, news which set the disappointed Luke cursing. The Devil, he thought bitterly, looked out for its own. Baldy also did some cursing.

'And I had the sonuvabitch in my sights, and missed him!' He shrugged. 'Still we've done ourselves proud here.'

'You and your boys better move out, Billy,' Luke said. 'All the firin' could be drawin' men here you'll not be overjoyed to meet up with. And thanks for your help. Without it we couldn't have wiped out this sidewinder's nest.'

Billy grinned. 'It helped to pass the time for us, Mr Culpepper. Better than sittin' on our asses drinkin' in some bar. And it's been a pleasure to have made your acquaintance.' He winked at Baldy. 'We'll get those cows and horses that're wanderin' about round-up and drive them towards Fort Sumner. It'll give Pat Garrett something to do; other than chase after us, he can sort out who they belong to.'

'Billy,' Luke said poker-faced. 'Far be it from me to try and lead youngsters off the straight and

148

narrow, but if I was you I'd drive those critters across into Texas. The money you get for them will pay for the shells you've used and tide you over for chow, or whatever, for the next few weeks. Count it as the reward the state owes you but you ain't in a position to get.'

'Why didn't you think of that, Billy?' Charlie Bowdrie said, wide-smiling. 'You reckon to be boss of this outfit.'

Billy pushed back his hat and scratched his head. 'I dunno, Charlie,' he said. 'M'be it's because I'm a river-baptized Christian and such sinful thoughts like cattle-liftin' ain't entered my head. It's sure got me puzzled.'

Baldy burst out into a cackling laugh. 'And m'be the hair will grow back on my head! Now go about your thievin' business before we all get religion!'

FIFTEEN

It was still a downcast and silent Luke who rode alongside his two *compadres*, keeping his own counsel on the trail to Fort Sumner. Baldy, seeing how disappointed Luke was at not having paid his beholden debt in full by killing Chato, tried to lift up his spirits.

'We did better than we could have honestly expected, Mr Culpepper,' he said. 'Did better than all those soldier boys who've been chasin' their asses all this time tryin' to hunt down Chato. We've cleared Chato outa his stronghold for good. Though the sonuvabitch slipped through our fingers, his raidin' days are over for a long spell, if not for good, bein' we wiped out most of his men.'

'Yeah, you're right, Mr Springer,' replied Luke shaking off his gloomy feelings. He thin-grinned. 'We didn't do too bad for three loco *hombres*. And young Billy and his boys were happy at the outcome. They're only a bunch of kids, but I ain't seen anyone enjoy killing as much as they did.'

Billy and his young *pistoleros* had left them back

151

along the trail, whooping and joking, to drive the sixty or so longhorns and horses east across into Texas for a quick, no-questions-asked sale.

'You boys take care of yourselves now,' Luke had told them when they were ready to move out. 'And thanks again for your help, we couldn't have pulled it off without your guns.' He grinned at Billy. 'If we meet the law on our way to Fort Sumner and they ask us if we know of your whereabouts, I'll tell them I ain't even heard of a *pistolero* called Billy the Kid.'

'I'd take kindly to that, Mr Culpepper,' Billy replied. 'I don't hanker having that long streak of a lawman Pat Garrett and his hangin' posse catch up with us herdin' these cows to the border.' Billy then stood up in his stirrups and yelled, 'Get these critters moving, boys!'

The three of them watched their former allies until all they could see of them was the trail dust of the cattle.

'I must have Injun blood in me, Mr Culpepper,' Baldy said. 'But I can smell death hangin' over those kids' heads.'

'They are takin' part in a war, Mr Springer,' Luke said. 'And men get killed in such-like activities. And we'd better keep a sharp eye out for any trouble on the trail, or we could end up bein' casualties in a war we know damn all about.'

'Mr Culpepper,' Campbell said, 'I'm disappointed as you we didn't send Chato to Hell, but we did our best. And an Eastern dude thanks you both for giving him back his self-respect – his very life for that matter.'

'You paid your debt back, Mr MacColl,' Luke said. 'By savin' two stupid old farts' necks with that sneaky pistol of yours. You're a good man to have walked the line with, Mr MacColl. Now ain't that so, Mr Springer?'

'I ain't the most sociable of characters, Mr MacColl,' Baldy said. Pick and choose who I ride with.' He grinned. 'There ain't no good reason for you stay here in New Mexico; Chato will be pushin' his horse across the Rio Grande by now to hole-up in Mexico someplace but if you're loco enough to step this side of the Pecos again and you want a pard, well, providin' me and Jethro are still movin' around, I'll ride with you.'

Campbell's face hardened suddenly. 'I'll have to make it east of the Pecos first, Mr Springer. And we've just picked up some company who could have a say in that. See!' He pointed behind his partners' shoulders.

Luke and Baldy twisted ass in their saddles and saw the line of hostiles. Luke swore. 'Well, I'll be damned! That's the same bunch who tried to hurrah us way back along the trail to Silver Butte to have words with you, Mr Springer.'

'And I sent that chief a message, a Sharps' slug close to his head, tellin' him not to mess about with us.' Baldy said. 'It seems he didn't read it right.' He drew out the Sharps. 'It looks that now they're all armed up with long guns they mean business this time.'

'And here's one of the red devils comin' at us!' Luke growled, pulling out his own rifle. 'It could be a young blood wantin' to prove his manhood. That

153

big gun of yours, Mr Springer, must still have them worried, the rest of them're keepin' their distance. What do we do, stand and fight here, or make a run for it? You're the Injun expert.'

For several seconds, Baldy keen-eyed the rider coming in at a walking pace before, he thought grimly, the son-of-a-bitch chose the moment to rib-kick his pony into a suicidal dash to claim a white-eye's scalp. Baldy sighed; he had tried hard not to have a war with the warband. He swung the Sharps up to his shoulder, only to quickly lower it again as a smile creased his face.

'It just goes to show, Mr Culpepper,' he said. 'It ain't wise to judge a fella too hastily. That ain't a young buck comin' in with blood in his eyes; though I ain't seen him before I reckon it's Mr Chato up on that horse. Is that so, Mr MacColl?'

'Good Lord!' Campbell gasped. 'You could be right, Mr Springer. Though I'll know for certain when I can get a closer look at his face.' He looked enquiringly at Baldy. 'But why? Why did the chief send Chato to us?'

'You're seein' an Injun honourin' his debt, Mr MacColl,' replied Baldy. 'Many of us white-eyes would find a way out of paying our debts; some have been known to kill rather than settle their dues. That chief is givin' us Chato's life for me allowin' him to keep his. He reasoned we must want Chato badly, or why would we attack his stronghold with so few men. You go out and bring him in, Mr MacColl, before the murderin' bastard falls off his horse. He don't look too steady in the saddle.'

154

Baldy raised the Sharps above his head, the peace gesture, then let out a bubbling Sioux victory call. Howling Wolf blinked his eyes in surprise. Who was this old white-eye, he thought, who knew the ways of the Indian? It was good they had not fought. He had the 'breed Chato's scalp, both his and the old white-eye's honour had been satisfied. He cupped his hands to his mouth.

Baldy grinned and lowered the Sharps as he heard the barking, wolf-like call. He saw the chief raise his own rifle above his head, then the war band turned away from them in a flurry of hoof-raising dust and rode south. He would liked to have passed the time of day with the chief, Baldy thought.

'Mr Culpepper,' he said. 'A half-crazy Eastern dude, a bunch of wild-ass kids, an Injun chief and an old man who oughta be sittin' in a rockin' chair on some front stoop, ain't much of an army, but it proved good enough for you to pay back what you felt you owed those poor Germans lyin' in those graves back there along the Pecos.'

'How the hell could we not pull it off, pard,' Luke said, smiling, 'when I had a mule taggin' along that could smell trouble as far away as the next county?' Face serious, he added, 'I'd like the kid to take Chato in, if it's OK with you?'

'It's OK by me,' replied Baldy. 'It'll buck him up no end, give him back his pride, if he ain't got it back already. And, as you said, if it hadn't been for the kid's quick thinkin', me and you wouldn't be havin' this conversation.'

'Mr Culpepper! Mr Springer!' they both heard

155

Campbell yell out as he reined-led Chato's horse towards them. 'Chato's been scalped!'

A shock faced Campbell drew up alongside them. 'It's Chato all right,' he said. 'He's hardly alive. Only being tied to his saddle has kept him on his horse.'

Luke and Baldy gazed impassively at the slouch-backed figure of Chato, and his bloodstained gargoyle's mask of a head.

'Yeah, I guess he's feelin' sorry for himself right now,' Baldy said. 'M'be reflectin' on his evil ways and all the grief and pain he's inflicted on folk in the state. Well, the rope round his neck at Fort Sumner will put an end to his pain this side of Hell.' He kneed his horse nearer to Chato's mount to take a closer look at the comanchero chief. 'Don't fret none, Mr MacColl,' he said. 'The sonuvabitch won't turn his toes up on us, he'll live to dance on air at Fort Sumner.'

They had been three days at Fort Sumner and seen Chato quickly paying for all his years of killing and robbing, the whole town turning out to see him hang. A wide-smiling Campbell told Luke and Baldy he'd had a Western Union wire from Alan Pinkerton offering him the post as field director at the new office the agency was opening at Fort Worth, Texas.

'I did promise myself,' he said, 'I'd never come west again if I remained a Pinkerton, but director is a position I can't turn down. I only hope I can hold the job down, Mr Culpepper.'

'Mr MacColl,' Luke replied, fatherly, 'you'll do just fine. In fact you have proved to me and Mr

156

Springer you're capable of commanding a company of Texas Rangers, and they come no tougher and more ornery than those *hombres*. You take the job with your ex-pards' blessin's.'

Campbell said his farewells to them then left to ride north to Sante Fe there to catch an east-bound train to Texas and his new post.

'I'm heading Texas way myself, Mr Springer, Big Springs,' Luke said. 'My old pa owned a piece of land there. I reckon it's more than a mite run down by now, but it's big enough to run several hundred head of cattle on it. You're welcome to make the trip with me, Mr Springer. You mountain men are expert cabin builders.' He grinned. ' 'Course, tendin' cows might be too quiet and peaceful for an old hell-raiser.'

'Mr Culpepper,' Baldy said, 'me and Jethro crave peace and quietness. We've been seekin' that since we drifted into New Mexico. Some men have a lustin' for women, some crave hard liquor, me – and I've never told this to anyone but Jethro before – I have a great longin' to be able to rest peacefully in a real bed, boots and clothes off, before I die. I'm too old for cold camps and tryin' to sleep on hard ground. And I reckon Jethro wouldn't curl up his lip at sleepin' in a barn. Mr Culpepper, I'll build you a fine cabin, tend woollies if I have to, my wanderin' days are over.'

'I'm pleased to hear that, Mr Springer,' Luke said. 'You're my first hirin'. Now let's get some supplies for the trail, pard, and get the hell outa Lincoln County in case we get dragged into young Billy's goddamned war.' He grinned at Baldy. 'We ain't got the Mole ridin' with us to pull us outa the crick if we get into deep water. We two old has-beens will have to fend for ourselves from now on in.'